Can't Fight the Mistletoe

JAYCEE WEAVER

Sandia Sky Press

Can't Fight the Mistletoe, ©2023 Jaycee Weaver

All Rights Reserved. No part of this book may be reproduced or transmitted in any form or by any means, electronic or mechanical, including photocopying, recording, or by any information storage and retrieval system without the written permission of the author.

Published by Sandia Sky Press LLC, Albuquerque, NM.

This is a work of fiction. Names, characters, places, and events are creations of the author's imagination or are used fictitiously. Any resemblance to actual persons, living or dead, events, or locations is purely coincidental. Some events and locations within Albuquerque, New Mexico are used with or without altering names and identities because the author loves her hometown and everything in it and intends absolutely no harm whatsoever. Any factual errors were made unintentionally or with creative liberties on my part to better further the story as necessary.

Table of Contents

Chapter 1 1
Chapter 2 7
Chapter 3 13
Chapter 4 22
Chapter 5 28
Chapter 6 34
Chapter 7 39
Chapter 8 45
Chapter 9 55
Chapter 10 62
Chapter 11 68
Chapter 12 75
Chapter 13 82
Chapter 14 89
Chapter 15 98
Chapter 16 107
Chapter 17 114
Chapter 18 121
Chapter 19 128
Chapter 20 135

Chapter 21 145
Chapter 22 152
Chapter 23 158
Chapter 24 166
Chapter 25 177
Acknowledgments 188

Chapter 1

Alessia

I've taken a lot of flak for rolling my eyes the past twenty-seven years—assuming I didn't learn how to convey irritation until age two. At this point, the action has become an unconscious and integral part of my personality.

Before you ask, *of course* I'm aware how rude and disrespectful it is. *Yes*, my mother raised me better.

Well, she tried. For a while.

I'm not trying to be disrespectful, but some people are just so dang stupid. Or annoying.

Or, as in the case of Danger Stevens, both.

Come on. *Danger Stevens*? His name alone triggers an eyeroll. Did no one think to tell his parents what a ridiculous name they were bestowing on their precious lastborn child? Perhaps they intended to upgrade it from a cheesy line (a la *Danger is my middle name*—accompanied by a smirk, wink, and inevitable finger guns) knowing it would be a hit with the ladies.

Because if there's one thing I know about the man, he is *definitely* a hit with the ladies. All the guy has to do is enter a room with his thick blond hair and gleaming smile, and *bam!* Anyone with two X chromosomes (and probably a few with a Y in there) perks to attention. Regardless of age.

I've watched it happen since middle school, through high school, then college, and presently at my place of work.

Take right now, for example. I don't have to glance over my shoulder to know what I'll see. Some female with pinked cheeks, tittering at the barest attention from one scruffy-faced Danger Stevens. Though, here at Valle Encantado Active Life Community, the woman's most likely over sixty.

Since I'm currently perched near the top of a five-foot A-frame ladder and facing the wall, I don't bother to hide my lip curl or eyeroll. Not that I usually do where Danger's concerned. He's well aware of my loathing for him. He likes to say it's *cute*.

Gross. As if any woman wants to be called *cute* past the age of ten. It's demeaning.

Gently tugging another pumpkin vine from the corner near the ceiling, I carefully wind the crepe paper greenery and place it onto my growing pile. I spent most of the morning removing hand-painted paper squashes and cornucopias from the facility's walls now that, as of yesterday, Thanksgiving is over. Three more feet and I'll be done.

Oops. I accidentally made eye contact. *Gah!* He has the nerve to wink. The man more than deserves a meme-worthy eyeroll for such audacity, so I happily comply before adding a saccharine smile and returning to my work.

As I reposition the ladder and begin the climb for the ninety-eighth time today, ignoring the disturbing age-gap flirtation happening behind me, I consider how I'll arrange the enormous ornaments, trees, and snowflakes I spent countless hours crafting last year. I'm anxious to see how they held up in the storage room I've only recently been given permission to reorganize.

I've itched to overhaul the mess for six years, but Danae preferred to organize her own way. As in, not at all. The woman was a fabulous activities director—able to juggle three months of mobility-encouraging social events and activities without dropping a single ball—but give her a purse, desk, or closet, and, well, good luck.

Me? I don't need luck. Organization comes as easily to me as a handspring to an Olympic gymnast. I'm that talented, too, which is why the board offered me the job when Danae declared her intent to retire and move to the humid sweat pit of San Antonio.

Why anyone would retire there is beyond me, though I guess it's not so different from Albuquerque, aside from the rampant humidity and population. Seriously, though, ew. I don't do humidity or crowds, but Danae seems fine with both. I'll keep New Mexico, thank you very much. Unless by some miracle there's a job in a small, non-humid beach town somewhere within driving distance of a mountain range with easy access to a Target and Hobby Lobby. *Ha!* Since that's never happening, I'll reside in Albuquerque until they lower my (hopefully) decrepit old corpse into the ground.

Ahem.

Apologies for the morbid moment. Today's been… a lot.

It started with a voicemail from my father followed by a guilt-inducing text of ambiguous tone from my mother. To avoid their drama, I told them both I'd be working over Thanksgiving and the weekend, so my money's on them each vying for dibs on Christmas.

And by "vying for dibs," I mean my dad offering to "let" Mom have this Christmas with me as the sacrificial good guy, and Mom suggesting I spend it with Dad because he doesn't get to see me often enough now he's moved to Nashville. Whatever. I'm smart enough to hear what they're not saying—they'd both rather focus on their new families than the reminder of their old one.

It's fine. I'm used to life on my own. I'll deal with them later. Besides, I'm at work, and my attention needs to remain focused on the task at hand and not whatever my dysfunctional train wreck of a family has on their agenda.

Right, so, work. *Sigh.*

The weight of my new position as Activity Director presses down on my shoulders as I remove yet another delicate vine from the wall using my handy dandy stick staple remover. I rotate my shoulders and stretch my neck. I'd love to close my eyes and do a bit of deep breathing, but the top of a ladder isn't exactly the wisest place for meditation.

One section left, I tell myself as I descend once more to add the bits of greenery to the growing pile.

"Need help, Alley Cat?"

I swallow a groan.

"Hello?" He snaps his fingers inches from my face. "Alley Cat?"

My hand shoots up and swats away the insulting digits while I throw him my very best glare.

"It's *Alessia*," I hiss, turning away and grasping onto the ladder for one last ascent. "And I'm fine."

"I like Alley Cat."

"I *prefer* Alessia."

"Nicknames not your thing?"

I throw him a frown over one shoulder. "I am not a feral feline."

"Walks like a duck, talks like a duck..." he trails off.

Without bothering to look, I know he's giving an unaffected shrug and smirk—signature moves. Plus, we've been performing some iteration of this since the sixth grade.

The realization drops on my head like the condensation beads clinging from the yellowed stain in the ceiling above me. I barely resist the urge to place a hand on my head to check for moisture.

Sixth. *Grade.*

I've been doing the same dance with Danger Stevens for going on eighteen years. Either he's next-level stupid, or he's the most persistent man to walk the earth.

"Or maybe I enjoy a bit of predictability in an otherwise unpredictable world."

The hand curled around the staple remover freezes mid-scrape. *He heard that?*

"You have a terrible habit of muttering to yourself, Alley Cat."

"Sometimes a girl needs intelligent conversation."

The final staple pops free, but I'm not fast enough, so the paper vine slides down the wall. He catches the strand between two fingers effortlessly, then proceeds to wind it into a perfect circle with surprising gentleness while maintaining thorough, smirking eye contact.

Why does God have to stack the deck for some people, hmm? Charm, confidence, *and* good looks—totally unfair for the rest of us.

"Thank you," I grit out, finally breaking his amused grayish-blue gaze.

"Difficult for you, wasn't it?" There's a smile in his voice that drives me batty.

"Everything is more difficult when you're around."

He emits a low humming noise in the back of his throat that sends a shiver from my neck down to my goosebump covered arms. Nuh-uh. It's only the breeze from the heater vent nearby. Danger Stevens is a flirt, just like Dad, which means I'm the last woman on earth he'd ever appeal to.

Plus, I've got way too much to accomplish here with only me to do the work. It's how I prefer to work.

"Don't you have someone else to pester? I'm busy."

He's undeterred, thanks to my mouth's inability to use a tone as harsh as my words.

"Everybody needs help now and then, Als. There's no shame in asking or accepting when you do."

I throw him an unimpressed look and resume my work. He releases a soft scoffing sound but goes on his merry way. Against my better judgment, I glance over my shoulder to watch his retreat.

His stride is missing its usual swagger, and for a moment I feel bad for treating him the way I do. Until he glances back and catches me staring, and his self-satisfied smirk is enough to absolve me from any guilty feelings. Somebody needs to keep that head of his from growing bigger than his body can support.

Danger Stevens doesn't know what he's talking about. I don't need anyone's help, certainly not his. I've essentially been on my own my whole life, and I'm totally fine.

Chapter 2

Dan

That woman, she kills me. So much attitude, so much animosity. For me. *Only* for me.

Not gonna lie, I kind of love it.

Before you get your shorts in a knot thinking I'm some kind of masochist, misogynist, or worse, let me clarify. I'm no fan of pain—mine or anyone else's. Also, not a tool who gets his kicks driving feisty women crazy. Nor am I, despite what Alessia Catano says, a skeevy Casanova who expects women to fall at his feet and those who don't are merely a challenge.

Womankind is a beautiful mystery, but as the only male raised in a household overflowing with females—my grandmother, mother, aunt, cousin, and three know-it-all sisters—I've seen behind the curtain. I have better insight to the frightening inner workings of the feminine mind than most men could handle. That's how I know Alley Cat only *thinks* she loathes me. If she bothered to get to know the actual me instead of making assumptions, her tune would change. Except she's not about to let that happen anytime soon, so I'll allow her to continue using me as a human scratching post.

For now.

A final glance over my shoulder sends me off with the satisfying view of Alessia's adorable scowl. She shakes her head, muttering to herself as she straightens her stack of paper vines and squashes. Not bothering to smother my grin, I head down the hall toward Silas's apartment.

He answers my knock with an incomprehensible grumble.

"You decent?" After last week, I have one hand over my eyes with my gaze firmly trained on the floor just in case. He's pretty fit for an old guy, but I didn't need to find that out firsthand.

"Don't be a baby. I had my shorts on."

"Baby? Pardon me if I don't consider three-sizes-too-big tighty-whities 'decent.' Or shorts, for that matter."

"I ain't got nothin' you ain't got, kid." Silas slaps my hand from my brow, shaking his head as he shuffles toward the living room. "For Pete's sake, you're blushing harder than a virgin on her wedding night."

Silas gestures toward the couch and plops onto the leather recliner he should've replaced a decade ago. He won't, though, because the mechanism still works. And while the seat's ripped to shreds, he finally got the cushion the way he wants it—worn to the shape of his butt. I'll take his word for it. The accidental peepshow last week burned a hole in my retinas that may never heal.

"Speaking of wedding nights..."

My head whips his way, terrified for the direction this conversation is headed, but Silas keeps talking without any mercy for the horrific images he's spawned in my brain.

"I'm gonna ask Peggy to tie the knot."

Whew. "Oh yeah? Somebody's a fast worker."

"At my age, son, you don't let the grass grow under your feet."

"Better under than over," I say with a shrug.

His raspy cackle brings a smile to my face. Silas has always had a warped sense of humor, and he was only too happy to help develop mine as well.

I was six or seven when we moved into my grandma's house. While my sisters helped Mom unload the truck, I stood at the end of the driveway munching an apple and staring at the old man across the street watering his bushes as though I'd never seen anyone use a garden hose before. The man nodded toward my Red Delicious, and I'll never forget his deadpan remark.

"They say an apple a day keeps the doctor away. I say an apple a day will keep anyone away if you throw it hard enough."

Took me a minute, but I got the joke, and he instantly became my favorite person. Grams warned me not to be a nuisance, but Silas eventually told her to mind her business—which was his way of saying he enjoyed having me for a shadow—and so began our friendship. He's a gruff old cuss, but he's the closest I've ever had to a granddad or father figure.

"What's your plan?" I ask, accepting the proffered Dr Pepper he retrieved from the mini fridge beside his chair.

"Kinda thought I'd just ask." Silas slurps his Diet Coke, grimacing at the can. "Ugh, I miss sugar. This stuff's nasty."

He's not wrong about the coke. But the proposal? No, sir.

"This is Peggy you're proposing to. The *one who got away*. The woman you loved, lost, and kicked yourself over for sixty years. Such a love deserves something special. You don't pop the question over a bowl of soup while watching the evening news."

"Soup and evening news, huh? What kind of schmuck do you take me for? We'd be having chicken and potatoes."

"Har har. Smart aleck."

"If you're such an expert, how would you do it?"

Expert, right. The closest I've come to proposing was my epic promposal fail senior year.

Early on, I wondered briefly whether my relationship with Santana had such potential, but God spared me before we got too serious.

"Dunno," I say after a while. "Make it personal. Meaningful."

Silas grunts but mulls it over. We spend the next hour kicking around ideas, and by the time I leave, he has a fairly decent plan in place.

"Thanks for the help, kid," he says with a clap on my shoulder. That's as good as a hug for him.

"Anytime, old man."

Alessia's nowhere in sight, but her ladder stands at the farthest end of the long hallway. The walls are bare now that she's removed the happy fall decorations, but if I know her, she'll have everything festive once more before nightfall. I've never met a more focused soul. Or one more independent.

A dozen memories of class projects and school activities come to memory as I stride toward the front desk and wave to Pam on my way out.

"See you next week, Dan," she calls with a merry singsong as the doors slide open.

Flashing her my best smile, I turn and walk outside backwards. "I'll be counting the days."

Pam's cheeks blossom at my wink. She's sweet. Reminds me of my aunt Mindy.

My beat up old 4Runner is unseasonably warm as I climb inside, a welcome reprieve from the chilly late autumn air. I've been spoiled by the warmer Texas temps these past few years, and it's going to take a while to get used to cooler weather again.

The weather isn't the only readjustment I'm facing, either.

Moving home to Albuquerque hasn't been the easiest transition. While growing up in the shallow end of an Olympic-sized estrogen pool fostered a deep appreciation and respect for all things female, sometimes a dude needs to be around other dudes. So, when I got recruited to teach at an all-boys high school in Dallas right out of college, I jumped at the chance.

And it was awesome. Until it wasn't.

Now I'm back, living across the street from my childhood home, spending way too much time with my family, and teaching English to a bunch of entitled charter school kids. Thanks to early dismissal Fridays, these weekly lunches with

Silas have become the highlight of my week, and not because they give me an excuse to run into Alley Cat. She's a bonus.

Tory's waiting on my front porch when I get home. We're what Grams calls Irish twins, Tory the elder by eleven whole months. I'm not surprised to see her, but I do wish my family would call before coming over. Oh well. I knew what I was in for when I bought Silas's house.

"Hey," she says before I'm fully out of the car. "How's Silas?"

"Same old."

Tory chuckles, restoring my smile. "I bet. Did he grill you about the yard?"

It's my turn to chuckle. "Not this time."

Silas is a man of few words, except when it comes to lawncare, Clint Eastwood, and the Old West. And lately, Peggy James. On a visit home this past Mother's Day, I saw the FOR SALE sign go up outside his house and feared the worst. I mean, the guy's pushing eighty. Thankfully, he came outside before I panicked and explained his decision to sell and move to Valle Encantado. Since I already knew my teaching contract wasn't being renewed, I didn't bat an eyelash about putting in an offer. Now I'm the proud owner of the house I spent most of my spare time in as a kid. A very dated, very western house with an enormous lawn.

"Did you show him your plans for the remodel?"

I flash Tory an incredulous look. "Of course not."

Silas has a hard time remembering it's no longer *his* house.

She laughs and follows me inside. I drop my laptop bag on one of the honey oak dining chairs I inherited with the house and dig through the fridge for a couple sodas. Tory accepts her preferred Sprite while I pop the top on another Dr Pepper. The sweet fizz burns so good.

"Ew!" Tory grimaces. "Do you always have to smack and sigh?"

"Nope," I give the *p* an extra pop. "Only on the first sip."

"Ugh. Boys are gross."

"Good thing I'm a man then, huh?"

"Are you, though?"

Sisters.

"So," she pauses in the melodic way that says she wants me to spill tea as if I'm one of her girlfriends. Since there's no stopping her when she wants something, I throw her a bone.

"Silas is proposing to Peggy."

She squeals, and I shove a finger in my ear to stop the ringing.

"For the love, Tor."

"Whatever. Tell me everything."

It's pointless to resist, so I do. By the end, she's grinning. "Guess this means you'll be seeing more of Alesssssia, then."

I swallow a groan at her taunt. Tory's had a front row seat to my and Alley Cat's complicated history. Leave it to her to sniff out my feelings. Still, I'm not about to confirm or deny when we both know Alessia will never give me a chance.

So, I play innocent. "How so?"

"Didn't you hear? Danae retired. If they're getting married at Valle Encantado, she'll be the one in charge of planning."

Boom. I figured out how to get Alessia to finally see me.

Chapter 3

Alessia

"He had the nerve to ask me if I was coming for Christmas. I was like, *uh, no*." My sister, Paige, scoffs through my earpiece. "Can you believe him?"

"Dad's never been the brightest candle in the box," I say while wrestling a ten-foot artificial blue spruce out of storage.

She laughs. "Truth. Seriously, though. He hasn't asked me to spend Christmas with him since the year my mosquito bites sprouted into real boobs. As if I'm going to trade Christmas with my mom for him? He's got his new wife and half a dozen other kids he can ask. Why me?"

My laugh quickly turns into a groan as I lurch forward, tripping over my own foot because the tree I'm fighting with got stuck in the doorway. I should probably get off the phone and tackle this problem, but whenever my sister calls, I answer.

Technically, we're half-sisters, but of the four—five? six?—siblings on our father's side, we're the closest. The rest are likewise being raised by their mothers in whichever cities our father had gigs over the last three decades. I'm not sure even *he* knows how many offspring he's spawned. Frankly, I don't care.

Hands on hips, I take a second to study the mass of fake greenery to figure out where it's hung up. Maybe with one. More. Solid. Shove—

"Are you okay?" Paige pauses her rant to ask.

My own rant is on the tip of my tongue. Why is the tree not inside a box with wheels?

Because *Danae*.

"Yup." Another grunt as I readjust and lean into it with my shoulder.

When I couldn't get out of spending the week after New Year's in Nashville for my dad's third wedding earlier this year, Danae did the undecorating by herself. I caught a glimpse of her handiwork in the storage room afterward and developed an eye twitch that lasted through Valentine's Day and has made a reappearance every holiday since.

Including this one.

No more, though. If I have to finance a plethora of storage bins out of my own paycheck, this space is going to be a glorious, stress-free thing of beauty by January first.

"I'm"—shove, groan—"*fine*."

"Oh my gosh, are you in the bathroom? Gross, Les! Have the courtesy to put me on mute."

"No, Paige," I sigh, giving up temporarily to catch my breath. "I'm at work, attempting to push an oversized Christmas tree through a door that is clearly *not* wheelchair width. I thought everything in this building was supposed to be universal design. I will *not* be defeated!" A primal sound, somewhere between a yell and a grunt, rips out my mouth.

"Sounds like you're giving birth."

"Ugh, thanks for that image."

This hallway echoes. What must the residents think?

"Now I'm going to be self-conscious the rest of the day." And avoiding eye contact like it's a disease.

Which, you know, I do often enough already.

She laughs, which lightens my mood and eases the ever-present knots in my shoulder muscles. Paige hasn't had an easy go of it, and she's far too serious and jaded for twenty-four. Anything I can say or do to ease her load—mentally, emotionally, spiritually—I'll do without a second thought. Her laughter's a reward I treasure.

"So," she says after a while. "Would you maybe want to go with me to Dad's for Christmas?"

"Ew. I saw him in January. Why would I go again?"

I give up and plop cross-legged on the storage room floor, wishing I liked coffee because my chai was useless this morning.

"Because he's our father?"

I make an ugly buzzer sound. Nothing she says will convince me to recreate the tension of *Four Christmases* with my sister.

"Try again."

"Because you love me?"

"True, but I'd rather fly you to me. We both know he'll probably cancel on us thanks to a last-minute gig or band crisis."

Our dad's not merely a charming, cheating flake, he's a musician too. Oh, and a first-generation Italian American whose personal mission is to perpetuate the stereotype Italian men are flirtatious womanizers. Except his father loved to coax a laugh from my grandmother, and while Nonno was certainly handsome and charismatic, he was faithful and head over heels for Nonna. So, I know it's not true for *all* Italian men.

Maybe just the charming ones.

Paige remains silent. Adjusting my grip on the stubborn tree, I wait for her to upgrade from asking to begging. She's nothing if not persistent. But her next question surprises me.

"Don't you think it's weird he's asking us to visit? I assume he asked you too."

Judging by her tone, she's worried about my feelings. She forgets that where our father is concerned, the only feelings I have are irritation. Everything else remains buried deep under a layer of rejection and drowned in the well of tears I refuse to shed.

"He left a voicemail on Friday, but I haven't listened to it yet. Why?"

"Dunno. He's never asked before."

"He hasn't actually asked me anything."

Her snort sparks a smile. "It's on your voicemail."

"I haven't *heard* anything. Come on, you should know bigger cases have been won on smaller technicalities."

This earns me a laugh, which is what I was going for as a nod to her final year of law school at UCLA.

"Fine," she relents. "If it works out, I'll come to you. But you'll have to find us a plausible excuse for Dad."

"Deal. I better run. This tree won't move itself." I don't hear her goodbye because my earbud tumbles to the floor at the same time said tree twists and shoots clean through the doorway.

"What the—"

"Thought you could use a little help, Alley Cat."

I groan, grumble, mutter, and swallow curses. "What do you want, Danger?"

"It's just Dan. Say it with me... *Dan*." He makes a show of forming the word with his dumb mouth. Two can play this game, though.

"And I'm *Alessia*," I repeat, nice and slow, for the four hundred and twenty-seven millionth time since childhood, adding "*Danger,*" with extra oomph.

Personally, I don't hate being called Als, Al, Lessi, or Les (though Alley Cat is the actual *worst*), but until he learns to use my proper name, I will continue to annoy him by using his.

He shakes his head with an irritatingly perfect smile before righting the tree in his grip. "Where do you want this?"

"I've got it. Don't you have somewhere to flirt—I mean be?"

"Aw, honey, there's nowhere I'd rather flirt than right here."

"Oh, is that why you're constantly here? Developed a taste for experienced, mature women, hmm?" I quirk one eyebrow.

"I can't speak to experienced, but I certainly wouldn't consider you *mature*, Als."

He's such a—

"*Ooh*, I earned an infamous Alley Cat eyeroll."

Good heavens, I'm going to end up with bulging eye muscles from these regular workouts if he keeps showing up.

"Two! I feel extra special. Now, where did you want this?"

He gives the tree a hard shake, and now I'll have to murder him. Those fake needles spread like glitter, and the janitorial staff here is passive aggressive enough after the confetti cannon debacle of 2021.

"Ugh," I sigh. "Fine. Let me grab the base first."

I dig inside the storage room for the broom and sweep the needles into a pile in the corner to vacuum later before hunting down the right tree base. It's up high on the opposite side of the room with the Easter stuff. Makes total sense, right? (Cue an eyeroll with accompanying headshake.) Once I have it in hand, I feel around for the keys clipped to my waist, kick the wedge from under the self-locking door, and let it slam closed on my way out.

Danger (*not* Dan) follows, his muscles straining against the fabric of his shirt as he carries the tree as though it weighs six pounds and not sixty, zigzagging through several corridors to our larger main dining room. It still smells like turkey and green beans in here, although Thanksgiving was four days ago. Then again, there's a decent chance they're serving it again since it's a popular entrée with this crowd.

"Let's put it over there." I point toward the gas fireplace on the wall cattycorner to the wall of windows overlooking the lawn.

"Well, aren't you sweet, helping our Lessi with the heavy lifting! And my, how... *capable*." Mrs. Sweeney from Building Four saunters into the room, beaming at Danger like he's a young Arnold Schwarzenegger.

Last I heard, he became an English teacher, not a bodybuilder. *Yeah, but if Mr. Stutz had looked like* that, *you'd have passed AP Lit with a perfect score.*

Shut up, brain.

I flash Mrs. Sweeney a polite smile, praying to the good Lord she doesn't reach out and squeeze the man's biceps. There's a disturbing gleam in her eye that makes me think she would.

"Just keeping myself off the naughty list, ma'am," he says with a wink.

For the love.

"'Tis the season and all."

She titters like a girl a quarter her age. "Where's the fun in that, sugar?"

Oh my word. Seriously?

"It is very sweet of him to help, Mrs. Sweeney, but we've got three more trees to move before he needs to skedaddle." *Buh-bye now. Hint, hint.*

Mrs. Sweeney leaves with a flirty remark I don't fully hear as I'm adjusting the tree in its base by myself, since Dan the Man is occupied. Once she's gone, he turns and gives me a raised eyebrow. I shrug and hightail it to the storage room for the next tree, but he's not done.

"*Skedaddle?*"

My bangs blow wildly with my huff. "You try spending forty plus hours a week around seniors and see if you don't pick up their lingo."

He chuckles. "Okay, you get a pass. My sister's a preschool teacher and says the same thing when we tease her about using *the potty.*"

Oddly enough, I feel less stupid. Turning with my keys in hand before unlocking the storage room door, I suck in a deep breath. Asking for help is so hard, and my body rebels against my next words.

"Do you mind assisting me with the other trees? If you're not too busy to lend your muscles."

"Noticed those, did you? Like what you see?" He smirks.

If he winks, I'm going to bruise him.

"Ew. No." *Liar.* "Can you help or not?"

He checks his smartwatch. "Sure. I'll have to be quick to get back before my next class, but it's fine."

I drag two of the six-foot trees out of storage and hand him one. "Are you sure? Is someone expecting you?"

Why else would he come to Valle Encantado on his lunch break? It's not Friday, which I've learned is his early dismissal day when he spends the afternoon with Silas Cooper in his apartment.

"Actually, I came to see you."

"Me?" *Why?*

He follows me toward the front desk, where I direct him to prop his tree on the left while I set mine in place on the right.

"Yes, you. Silas wants to propose to Peggy James, but he needs something better than slipping a ring into her drink at dinner."

"And you want my help?"

"Yeah, I had a few ideas, but you're the activities person now, so—"

"Director." At his puzzled frown, I add, "Activity *Director*." Maybe not an important distinction to anyone else, but the title matters to me.

"Sorry, Activities *Director*, so I wanted to run it by you and—"

He's cut off by a booming voice. "Danny Boy! Thought I saw your vehicle in the lot. Shouldn't you be reading *The Great Gatsby* to a bunch of twerps right now?"

Danny Boy grins. After hearing that gem, so do I. The older man stands inside the sliding doors holding Ms. Peggy's hand. They're also smiling, only theirs is the kind that glows with the joy of true love. According to movies and books, anyway. I've never seen it in real life, so I can't say for sure.

"It's *For Whom the Bell Tolls* this time, and I'm on lunch. Thought I'd enlist Ms. Catano here for the project we discussed last week."

Mr. Silas waves his free hand in the air. "Oh, I already took care of that this morning."

"You what?" Danger's voice pitches upward in surprise.

"Told ya I had it covered." He lifts their joined hands, pointing to a lovely antique-set jade ring with a diamond chip in the center.

"Congratulations!" I rush to hug Ms. Peggy, whose smile is glowing so bright it's practically neon.

"Please tell me you didn't ask her while watching the morning news," Danny Boy deadpans.

Yes, I'm totally adding that to my nickname repertoire now.

Mr. Silas grunts while Ms. Peggy laughs.

"It was perfect, Dan," she says as he bends in half to hug her small frame.

Dan releases her and steps to the side where I'm repositioning the second tree. I don't want to be rude, but also don't have time to dillydally.

"We went for a walk in the park," Ms. Peggy begins. "'A stroll down memory lane,' he said," she giggles. "We reminisced about the first time we dated, then he stopped to sit at a park bench. He said his greatest regret would always be letting me go, not fighting hard enough to stay together. He missed sixty years he should've spent with me and didn't want to waste another sixty seconds. Then he dug this ring out of his pocket and asked me to marry him!"

You always hear the term "blushing bride," and now I see why. Ms. Peggy's face glows bright and lovely, with the apples of her cheeks turning the prettiest pink as she tells the story of her happiest moment.

My eyes sting.

"I'm so happy for you two," I say around the bubble in my throat. Despite my doubts about love, proposals always make me a little emotional.

"Thank you! And I'm so glad you're both here because we're going to need your help."

Wait a second. Did she say—

"Both?" Dan asks.

"Yes! My first husband and I went to the courthouse. Silas promised me the wedding of my dreams this time, and I always wanted to be married in style! It's going to be all hands on deck."

"Oh, I'll be fine on my own," I assure her. "Danny Boy can't take time away from his students. Have you set a date?"

"The day after Christmas."

No no no no no.

My mind races, formulating a dozen arguments against helping plan a wedding. My already overflowing calendar of holiday events and the minutiae it takes to pull them off. The myriad of other responsibilities that come with the activity director's job. Getting the storage room organized. Work-life balance, which I'm already lousy at.

Where am I supposed to find the time or the energy?

Ms. Peggy's countenance glows. She's so happy and earnest in her request, I don't have the strength to refuse.

"I'll have plenty of time," says the ever-so-helpful man beside me. "My winter break begins December thirteenth."

He turns to me with that sideways smirk I loathe. "Als, if you'll get the ball rolling, I'll be yours for two whole weeks."

I barely suppress my groan. There's no way out of this, even if I found the gumption to tell a sweet old lady no. Which I never will. Guess I'm adding *wedding planner* to my resumé.

Maybe a little help wouldn't be the worst idea.

Does it have to be Danger Stevens, though?

Sigh.

At least now I have a legitimate excuse not to visit Dad for Christmas.

Chapter 4

Dan

In hindsight, when Ms. Peggy said she wanted to be married *in style*, we should have asked questions.

"What exactly does *in style* mean?" for starters.

Better yet, I should've politely declined Ms. Peggy's request for my help and run out of there like my beard was on fire.

"We are not giving them a western-themed wedding. She said *in style*, not western style!" Alley Cat fumes, her gaze narrowed, muscles coiled, ready to claw my eyes out.

"Silas loves westerns. He lives for them, and it's *his* wedding too." I cross my arms and stand taller for effect.

While it's true Silas loves old westerns with a level of dedication a younger generation might term *fanboy*, the man has given no indication as to what sort of wedding he envisions. Not something men typically waste brainpower on. But when I arrived on yet another lunch break slash prep period (the truest sacrifice, as any educator knows) ten minutes ago, something inside me snapped. Alessia's tiny office resembles the wedding aisle at a thrift store gone wrong.

I *had* to speak up.

For Silas.

"They're getting married the end of December," she huffs, "which is my second busiest month of the year. The entire place is already half decorated for the holidays, and adding elegant touches of white will be simple and stylish." Her inflection emphasizes *stylish*, but her brows stress the first word.

She needs this to be simple or she'll lose her ever loving mind. Got it. Except—

"What if Peggy doesn't want a wedding that looks like Valentine's Day and Christmas threw up inside a bridal magazine?" I challenge.

Alessia rounds the desk, mirroring my stance so close I see she's got a booger flake flickering on each irritated exhale. I smother my grin with a subtle nose rub. She pointedly glares from my hand to the oversized pump bottle of hand sanitizer on the corner of her desk.

Oh, *she's* worried about *my* snot when she's got a boog the size of Rhode Island?

Wisely, I keep my mouth shut and pump a generous amount of sanitizer into my hand, making a show of rubbing it in nice and careful without breaking eye contact.

She rolls her eyes with a trademark huff. "It's chaotic in here because I wasn't sure what Ms. Peggy wanted, so I went into storage and brought out everything we've used for past weddings. Which, admittedly, is no small amount."

"Ah. That explains the bells. I'm guessing the height of style for weddings in 1985?"

They're hideous. The once-white hard plastic is a dingy yellow. The top is tied with a crumpled mass that I assume was red velvet ribbon at one time but is now the shade of dried blood.

Alessia huffs through her nose, dislodging the bat from its cave, which goes flying onto the bells. She freezes, staring at the dry flake in horror. Her face blanches before turning completely red. I've never seen a human this red aside from sunburns. She springs into action, grabbing the bells and launching them into the wastebasket at the end of her desk.

"I'm also cleaning out the storage room. Clearly."

My family's efforts to raise a gentleman kick in, and I purposefully examine a set of silver candlesticks like an expert appraiser, all the while watching her frantically sanitize her own hands in my periphery. She glances my way three or four times, but I wait until her face returns to a normal shade before angling my body toward her.

I saw nothing. Nothing at all.

It's harder than it should be to keep my lips from twitching, though. She's always been adorable when she's mad, but blushing and hiding the evidence of her humanness? Might be my new favorite.

She's just always so poised. Completely put together and perfect with everything flawlessly organized and precisely ordered for as long as I've known her.

Maybe that's why seeing her office a mess today threw me off.

Or maybe it was all the lace.

I shudder, searching the room for anything remotely masculine among these piles of white and fluff.

There. A cowboy boot. Plucking it from under a pile of faux pearl strands, I realize it's a vase for flowers, but it'll help me paint the scene for something far more fun than a typical, classic Christmas wedding.

"A Western theme can be elegant too, and simple if we do it right. I mean, check out how cool this boot shaped vase is."

"It's really not. I think it's a relic someone made in Jobie March's art class ten years ago." She points to the pile of assorted ugliness. "You're in my pitch pile. *Not* the wedding pile."

I shoot her a look. "Humor me. How long would it take to remove the Christmas stuff from the chapel and reception area? A few hours?"

She scoffs. "It took me a whole week to decorate! You think I can tear everything down in a few hours and transform the space into an old western saloon like that?" Her fingers snap.

I shrug. "What, move a few trees, some wreaths, and a few sprigs of mistletoe?"

The sound she produces is part scoff, part snort. It's adorable.

Then thoughts of mistletoe and what it stands for remind me of thoughts I haven't had for this woman in years. *Shut it down, man.* I'm here for Silas and Peggy, and nothing else.

"I'll pitch in. It'll be easy." I only need mention it to my family, and they'll have a whole crew here to finish the job in an hour.

"Absolutely not."

"Fine. Then I guess there's only one way to solve this."

"You leave me alone and let me handle it my way?"

I chuckle. "Nope. We ask the bride and groom what *they* want."

"Fine." Alessia drops the string of pearls she'd been running through her fingers and marches through the door.

She doesn't stop marching (stomping, really) until we reach Ms. Peggy's apartment. No one answers, so I follow her down two floors to Silas's.

The pair answers after a long minute, breathing heavily. The corner of my mouth fights to tilt upward as I take in the piece of Silas's thin gray hair sticking up in the back and the smudge of lipstick on Peggy's upper lip.

"Y'all need a chaperone?" I drawl with a smirk.

Silas glares. Ms. Peggy's cheeks flush pink. But Silas throws an arm over her shoulder and kisses her cheek. They both grin with no shame over being caught making out like teenagers.

"Not necessary," Peggy says, regaining her usual poise. "Now, to what do we owe this... unexpected visit?"

"Wedding!" Alessia shouts. She clears her throat before speaking in a normal tone. "We had some ideas for the wedding we needed to run past you."

"Oh! Wonderful!" Peggy swings the door wide and motions for us to come inside. "We've been talking, and Silas and I have agreed on a theme."

Ha! I knew it.

"Th-theme?" Alessia sounds worried, which makes it both imperative and impossible to fully smother my grin.

She takes a seat on Silas's couch, scooting to the corner. Ignoring her intention to sit as far away from me as possible, I plop right onto the middle cushion, recline with both arms spread across the low back of the ancient couch, and kick one leg up to rest over the opposite knee. I'm the picture of ease to counter her stiffness. Spine so straight she might as well be wearing a brace, she has both feet flat on the floor, hands crossed neatly in her lap.

"Yes, it's going to be everything I ever dreamed of!" Ms. Peggy clasps her hands over her heart. "Silas and I often spent Saturday nights at the cinema when we dated the first time around."

Satisfaction ripples through me. Wow, I love being right, especially when I was goofing around with the idea and not the least bit serious. Lucked out on that one. I'm about to elbow Alessia and mime a mic drop when Ms. Peggy clarifies.

"I always dreamed we'd run away and get married by the ocean," she gushes with a happy sigh. "A tropical wedding like Joan Blackman and Elvis Presley's in *Blue Hawaii*."

Huh? I glance at Alessia. She's staring at Ms. Peggy as though the woman announced she wanted to be married to Elvis himself. On Mars.

"I–I'm sorry, what?" she says after several vacant blinks.

Can't blame her. I'm equally stupefied.

"Well, obviously, we're too old to be running off to get hitched on the beach, so we'll do it here. At Valle Encantado."

"You want a tropical wedding. At Christmas. In *New Mexico*?"

Alessia's stuck, but I'm already pushing ahead full steam, calculating how much help we'll need to pull off something so insane. Sure, messing with her about a cheesy theme wedding was fun earlier when it was a joke, but I see the stress in her eyes.

There's no way she'll be able to handle her regular job during the holidays and arrange an over-the-top wedding too.

She'll try. That's what Alessia does—everything, perfectly. By herself. Trust the guy who worked with her on enough group projects in school.

"With Elvis for our officiant." Peggy adds earnestly.

I send a wide-eyed glance to Silas for confirmation. He's giving Peggy an indulgent smile unlike any I've ever seen on the old man's face.

"But—"

Alessia's protest is cut off by Silas's raspy voice. "If the love of my life wants a beach wedding here at home officiated by Elvis the day after Christmas, that's what she will have."

"Of–of course," Alessia rushes to agree. "Are we firm on the date? Perhaps late spring outside would be—"

"December twenty-sixth." The tone Silas uses kept me in line over half my life, including the mouthy middle school years.

I'm tied between being proud of Alessia for trying to put her foot down and finding humor in her hard swallow as she understands what I've always known—there's no winning an argument with Silas Cooper.

Nor, apparently, Peggy James.

In unison, Alessia and I give the only logical response.

"Yes, sir."

But I know another thing Alessia doesn't. She won't have to do this alone. Even if she thinks she needs to.

Chapter 5

Alessia

"I may have to quit my job, Audrey."

Her warm brown eyes stare unblinking, silently waiting for my rant to end.

"Yes, I barely got the promotion, but it's not worth the headache. Who cares if I'd have to move in with Mom and Gerald? Well, Mom might. Though, she might be okay with it since they'll have a live-in babysitter again..."

Audrey and I both know I'll never quit. I've worked too hard to get this far, and while it's not exactly a lucrative career, I've been happy at Valle Encantado. Besides, Mom's high expectations programmed a hyperdeveloped sense of responsibility within me, probably to compensate for the loose cannon who contributed the other half of my DNA.

"No, you're right," I continue. "I can't quit. I stink at babysitting. And besides, Mom will never let you come with me, and I love you too much to say goodbye."

My five-year-old chestnut agouti mini-lop, Audrey HepBun, pokes her twitchy nose into the blanket nest I've created in my lap. She turns a circle before doing the same to my chest. I run a hand down her head, loving the way her soft fur feels under my fingers. People say dogs are man's best friend only because they've never had a rabbit. Part bestie, part pet, one hundred percent emotional support animal. No dog could soothe my nerves the way Audrey does.

Better than any therapist, she's already listened to me rant about the cowboy wedding Danger proposed, as well as a detailed rundown of my closet reorganization slash wedding planning fiasco today. I owe her a handful of cabbage and an hour running around the escape-proofed backyard after this.

Once she's settled inside her hutch on the porch, I venture to the kitchen in search of sustenance, only to be reminded by my nearly empty fridge and cupboards I neglected to do my usual Monday night grocery run. This week I was reeling from an impromptu wedding announcement and worked two hours later than usual making a list that rivals Santa's. Only instead of naughty and nice, I'm checking my to-dos twice.

I'm not a wedding planner. In fact, had I known how much of my day-to-day would be spent helping Valle Encantado residents with their love lives, I'd have gone running for the hills. Why didn't Danae warn me about this part of the job, huh?

At no point during my interview process, nor in the totality of my time working under Danae, did anyone warn me I'd be working on a live set of *The Golden Bachelor*.

I wish I'd pitched the idea to the network when I first thought of it. Could've made a fortune and retired three decades early. Think about it. Valle Encantado is a beautiful setting with a large group of single seniors living in close proximity to a pool. Plus, they already turn my planned events into group dates. Instead of roses, they could give out, like, bingo cards or something.

Where was I going with this?

I don't know. Maybe my brain's reached a breaking point.

Clearly, I need food. *Stat.*

After double checking the back door is locked, I grab my keys and hit the Burqueño Burger drive-thru on the way to the store. The green chile cheeseburger will no doubt give me heartburn, but I can't bring myself to care. It's the only food I've eaten since the bagel I swiped from our on-site café this morning. One of these days, I'll get smart and meal prep for myself.

If only I were as organized in my personal life as I am for work. *Sigh.*

A prime front-door parking space opens up (score!). The place is a total ghost town inside. Praise God for small miracles, since I am dead sexy right now. The first thing I did when I got home from work was ditch the bra before changing into my favorite joggers and oversized hoodie—both of which are ancient and more than likely sporting stains of unknown origin under a layer of rabbit hair.

The first cart I grab has a squeaky wheel, so I move to the second line of carts and try again. I've made a decent-sized dent in my shopping list and budget when a familiar masculine voice brings me to a halt. I can't see him yet, but their voices tell me Danger Stevens is with a woman.

Shocker. *Ugh.*

"No, Mave," he says, voice firm and sure. "You can't have brownies."

"Rude!" The female voice retorts. "Never tell a woman what she may or may not eat."

You tell him, girl.

"What's next? I still have papers to grade."

He's seriously not going to address his faux pas? No apology?

"Ice cream, pickles, and mayonnaise," the woman says as if reading from a list. "Oh, and potatoes."

Danger chuckles. "The actual list. Not your cravings, woman."

"Don't call me *woman*."

The corners of my mouth edge upward. I should be making a beeline for the checkout line, but I can't help my curiosity. Who is this person? She's unlike his usual fan club of gigglers and hair twisters.

"Cravings *are* my list. And fine, I'll forego the brownies and ice cream, but don't you dare get between me and my potato salad."

"But Mave, you're—"

"Danger Immanuel Stevens, so help me," the woman says with absolute authority. "If you end that sentence with *fat*, or any other comment about my weight, I will end you. Now get. Me. My. Pickles."

"Yes, ma'am."

Stifling a chuckle, I push my cart forward. It's getting late, and I've got to get these groceries home before the ice cream I ought to skip (but won't) melts.

"Alley Cat."

I freeze, only now realizing I'm standing in front of the pickle shelves. Wonderful.

"Danger."

"Just Dan."

"That's not what she called you," I say with a smirk, jabbing a thumb toward the next aisle. "Immanuel, huh? *God with us.* Did your mom take one look and say, 'this kid needs to come with a warning label'?"

"Oh, I like her," the woman with him snickers as she rounds the corner.

By now I recognize her voice, but as she comes into view, I'm not sure why she's so familiar when I've never seen her before. She comes to a stop beside Danger and my gaze catches on her swollen midsection. The man's a charmer, but I never pegged him for—

"Mave, this is Alessia Catano. Als, my sister Maverick."

Oh. Okay, now I get the familiarity. They share the same wavy dark blond hair and grayish blue eyes. Hers are filled with the same teasing glint, too, though she's about three inches shorter and lacks the beard (for which I'm sure she's grateful).

"Hi," I say after too long.

I know I should say more, but nothing's coming out. Instead, I'm standing here like an idiot cataloging the other features they share, such as the twitch at the right corner of their lips as they smother smiles. I'd wager my pint of mocha Oreo their grins are identical.

This is weird. I'm being weird.

Can you blame me, though? I've been caught eavesdropping on Danger Stevens in my sweats with no bra, and now I'm meeting his sister. His very pregnant sister.

"So, this is the infamous Alley Cat, huh?" she says with a smile that confirms my suspicions.

Man, I'm glad I didn't place any actual wagers because I really want my ice cream. Correction, I *need* it after today.

Also—did she say infamous?

My gaze darts to her brother, who avoids my gaze and studies the rows of pickles. His cheeks are beet red above the scruff of whiskers outlining his jaw as he reaches for a jar of spears, hesitates, and grabs a jar of dill relish with the other.

"These okay?" He extends both to Mave, who raises an eyebrow and nods toward the cart. He complies, deliberately avoiding my eyes.

Interesting. Does this mean he's talked about me? I'm not entirely sure how I feel about that.

"*She* gets ice cream," Mave says, pointing to my cart with a pout.

My lips twitch. I'd say she's a couple years older than us, early thirties-ish, but her tone is reminiscent of my mom's youngest, who's six.

Danger tilts his head and gives her a pointed look. "*She* doesn't have gestational diabetes."

"Whatever." Mave crosses her arms with a humph.

My smile breaks free at their interaction. Here I thought he was being a body-shaming jerk, but it turns out he's a good brother watching out for his sister.

It's cute.

Smile gone. Danger Stevens is a pain in my butt. He's a flirt. A charmer. He's a lot of things that drive me crazy, but cute is not one of them.

Except then he gives her an indulgent smile reminding me so much of the one Silas gave Peggy earlier today, a tiny piece of my heart melts.

Danger Stevens took his pregnant sister grocery shopping after work.

Another sliver melts.

Stupid sliver.

Fine, okay? Maybe he's *a little* cute.

Chapter 6

Dan

"So…"

Have to give Mave credit for making it a whole four minutes into our drive home from the store.

"Oh, come on," she prods from the passenger seat of my 4Runner. "It wasn't so bad."

"*Infamous*, really?" I shoot her a glare before returning my focus to the road. "And you cornered her into giving me her number."

She laughs, a sound I've missed these past five months. Longer, if you count the years I lived in Texas. But in the five months since her husband's death and my move home… let's just say hearing her laugh twice tonight gives me hope she'll be all right. Even if her laughs came at the expense of my dignity.

"She's pretty."

"Mmm." I'm not giving her more.

"Oh, come on. Don't be a baby."

"A baby? You made me look like a pimple-faced tween with a crush and no game." Hearing the whine in my tone, I cough and drop an octave. "I'm plenty capable of getting a woman's number if I want it, thanks."

"Oh please," she brushes a hand through the air. "If it makes you feel better, I think she's into you."

I scoff. *Right*. Alessia has never once, not ever, been into me. Still... women are rarely wrong about these things.

"How can you tell?"

"Ha! I *knew* you liked her."

Outmaneuvered by my sister. *Again*. I have a sudden urge to fake getting lost and then prove I don't need to ask for directions. Grunt. Bench press a car.

"You're the worst, Mave."

"All right," she relents, albeit with a teasing tone. "I'll tell you. But only because I know you've had a crush on her since middle school."

"That's ridiculous."

"Don't play dumb with me, Danny. You think I don't remember how red your face would get when Tory teased you about your *Alley Cat*? Or the way she'd air claw and hiss whenever Mom asked about girls you liked?"

I groan. "That was a long time ago."

No need to tell her those old feelings came roaring back with a vengeance the first time I ran in to Als this summer while getting Silas moved in. I passed her in the hallway and instantly recognized the long, dark waves cascading to the sway of her back as she stapled something to the wall. She didn't see me thanks to the pile of boxes I carried, but I promised myself I'd say hi once I'd showered and no longer smelled like a monkey.

The next day, Alessia had stopped by to welcome Silas to the community and give him a copy of the July activity calendar. Just my luck, the pizza delivery girl showed up at the same time. It was one smile—*one*—to be nice, and the girl giggled and flirted with me the entire time it took Silas to find his wallet. He insisted on buying or I'd have used my card and avoided the entire encounter.

"Some things never change, I see," Alessia had said with her usual eyeroll and snark.

So much for a second chance at a first impression. My fate was sealed, and it's been high school revisited since.

I pull the SUV into Mom's driveway to ease unloading for Mave. She could cross the street if I parked at my place, but the floodlights illuminate the fatigue in the shadows under her eyes.

"Go on inside. I've got the bags."

She nods with a yawn. "I should argue, but I won't. Thanks, little brother."

You know Mave's tired when she waits for me to round the vehicle and get her door. As much as they drilled the habit into me growing up, she's always been the one to insist if a woman wants to open her own door, a man should let her and not get offended about it. Same with paying for dinner, though I've yet to lose that battle.

"Her snark is a mask, Dan," Mave grits through her clenched teeth as she accepts my hand and strains to unfold herself from the front seat. "She doesn't want to like you, but she does, and it drives her nuts. So, she's mean to you."

My smile appears at her words. It's nice to have my suspicions confirmed by a female. Maybe *hopes* is the more accurate word. Either way, I'm standing taller now than in the canned foods aisle.

"Ugh. To think I have two more months of this." Mave groans, rubbing her lower back.

She waddles inside as I pop the lift gate and start slipping the handles of the reusable shopping bags Mom has us use over my arms. Mave's nowhere to be seen by the time I lug everything inside.

"My hero!" Mom exclaims at the sight of my full armload, her exaggerated swoon putting a huge grin on my face.

I drop the bags on the island before accepting her hug.

She pats my shoulder blade, snickering. "There's my smart guy, getting everything in one trip like I taught you."

This has been our dance since I joined the ranks of licensed drivers. She's always hated grocery shopping. Scout and Mave did it until they went off to college, then it was me and Tory. Sometimes Aunt Mindy and my cousin Candice would handle it, but more often than not, it's me and whoever is free at the time.

Considering it earns me free meals on nights I don't feel like cooking for one (which is most), it works out.

"Where's Mave?" Mom glances behind me.

"Getting ready for bed, I hope." I meet Mom's concerned gaze and give what I hope is a reassuring smile. "She's tired, but in a normal way. Actually got her to laugh a couple times."

Mom's shoulders relax as she leans against the counter with a sigh of relief. "You're good for her. I'm so glad you're home."

"Glad to be here."

"I know it wasn't easy, leaving the life you'd built behind. But have I said lately how grateful I am you did?"

She has no idea how easy leaving Texas truly was, and I have no desire to correct her assumptions.

"Family comes first, Ma. You taught me that. Trust me, it was no great hardship."

There's no opportune time for something as awful as death, but Brian's passing brought me home at a time when I needed my family as much as they needed me. I hate that my sister is grieving, and especially that Brian's gone. He was a good man, a great brother-in-law, and the best partner to Mave. It sucks he won't be here to see his baby born, to watch him or her grow up, and it's not fair for the baby to never know their father.

I don't understand why God allowed it to happen, but I've long since stopped asking God why He does anything and try instead to accept He knows the plan even when it makes no sense to the rest of us.

"Hungry?"

I chuckle. "No, Ma. You fed me two and a half hours ago, remember?"

"Which is why I'm asking. Been filling your hollow leg since puberty."

"I'm good, thanks. Gonna head home. Papers to edit, tests to grade."

"Books to read," she adds with a wink.

Moms always know the truth. I shoot her an innocent grin on my way out of the kitchen, stealing a handful of cookies from the plate she left there especially for me. My students' papers will still be there waiting after I indulge in a few chapters of the Garrett Wilson novel I've been reading.

After reparking the 4Runner in my own driveway across the street, I put away the contents of my single canvas sack and flop onto the couch, phone in hand. I'd give my left arm for a recliner like Silas's, but I'm still rebuilding my savings after the move. While I'll have to wait a while for a throne of my own, I don't have to wait to contact Alessia now that I have her number. To ensure she has mine in case she needs it, that's all.

Fresh humiliation over my sister's antics—Maverick living up to her name, as always—washes over me as I tap the phone screen to search for Alessia's contact. Takes a minute of scrolling, but when I reach the letter N, I burst out laughing.

Not a Feline

I knew from the slight upturn of her lips she'd saved her number under something besides her name. When I click the message icon, I notice she already sent herself a text. The message reads Mr. Warning Label.

It's enough to know she has my number. Grinning, I put my phone away and crack open my book, ready to find out who this Trevor Delgado guy is and whose side of the fight he's on.

Chapter 7

Alessia

It's days like today that tempt me to try coffee again. But no matter how many times I've tried, my tastebuds flat refuse to adapt to the flavor of burnt bean water. With or without cream and fancy flavor syrups. Tea alone doesn't pack enough punch. It's the first Friday in December, though, which means it's officially peppermint cocoa season. I made do last month with caramel cocoa and the occasional cider, but there's nothing like the opposing flavors of hot cocoa and cool mint to reinvigorate me when the afternoon lag hits.

"Here you are, Pam. One medium peppermint mocha."

She beams as I set the hot paper cup on the twinkle-lit front desk. We share an affinity for peppermint and chocolate during December (maybe January, but it feels wrong any other time of year). Except, unlike me, Pam adores coffee.

"You're an angel," she sighs after her first sip. "Exactly what I needed to get over the three p.m. slump."

She yawns, which of course means I follow, because who can even *read* the word "yawn" without their mouth stretching wide and a wave of sudden fatigue cresting over them? Not that I read. Who has the time?

"Ugh! Don't start yawning, we'll never stop."

She snickers at my follow-up yawn.

Seriously, the three o'clock slump is legit. Especially after a night like mine where Audrey HepBun woke me at four thumping her foot against the bottom of her hutch in warning to the neighbor's free-range cat. Thankfully, I was able to resettle for two more hours of sleep. Since I'm staying for tonight's holiday kick-off activity, I'd already planned to come in later.

"Are we set for tonight's movie?"

Pam confirms, and I say a prayer of thanks the maintenance crew didn't object to an event involving popcorn and bowls of bite-sized candy. But come on, how do we usher in the holiday season with a Christmas movie and *not* serve the requisite accoutrements? I'll more than likely wind up sweeping the floors anyway to save myself their side-eye.

The sacrifices I make for this place.

Not ready to face my tiny office and the clutter I've yet to disperse, I spend a few minutes adjusting the spacing on the swags of twinkle lights hanging from the front desk. The trees on either side came out great, but she could use a little something on the wall behind the desk. There might be a spare set of stars and a wreath in the closet. I haven't had the time to finish decorating since my focus has been divided between our usual group activities, wedding checklists, and tackling the devil's closet.

"Afternoon, ladies. How are you this fine Friday?" The man sounds like a character from one of Paige's regency novels.

"Hi, Dan!" Pam says, chipper as always.

Traitor. Who brought her the mocha, hmm? Where's the loyalty?

"Alley Cat."

I turn to face him, an arch to my brow. "Not a feline, Danger."

"Just Dan."

"I'll get it right when you do." I give him a saccharine smile while fluttering my eyelashes sarcastically. It's a special skill I'm thinking about adding to my resume, right below eyerolling. What can I say? I'm good with my eyes.

"What's showing tonight?" He changes the subject without acknowledging my exceptional talents. *Rude.*

"Last I checked, you're under fifty-five and therefore ineligible to be part of the Valle Encantado community."

"Never took you for an ageist, kitty."

Since it's a bad idea to affirm his nickname choices by clawing him to death literally, I choose the high road of ignoring him.

"Now, now, children," Pam teases. I'd forgotten she was here. "Of course, Dan is welcome. After all, he's still checked in as Silas's guest. And Dan, we're watching *It's a Wonderful Life*."

"A true classic," he says, nodding as if he knows.

I bet he's never actually seen it.

"Although," he continues, "if I had to choose between it and *White Christmas*, the latter is far superior."

Color me impressed. I never would have pegged Danger Stevens as a classic film fan. It takes a special kind of patience these days to sit through a long, slow-moving black-and-white (yes, it's been colorized, but don't get me started on *that* subject), even if it is one of the greatest movies of all time.

And a musical? Well, that's a rare man indeed. Of course, just because he's seen both doesn't mean he's among those *truly* rare and special.

Movies are my first language. But is he fluent in geek?

"I would agree *White Christmas* is the superior *Christmas* movie." Before he gets too comfortable in his self-satisfied smile, I continue. "However, Capra's is the superior *film*."

"Oh? How so?"

Am I glad he took the bait. This is one argument I will never lose. While he was busy getting his English degree, I was dual majoring in therapeutic recreation (for my career) and film studies (for my soul).

"For one, *It's a Wonderful Life* isn't a Christmas movie."

Pam groans. She's heard my rant on this subject since the year I began assisting Danae. The same movies slide onto the calendar year after year by request of the residents. Once, I tried to show *Elf*, and you'd have thought I planned to incite a riot. But this one?

He protests. "It tops nearly every Christmas movie list!"

Exactly that.

I clear my throat and crack my neck side to side, giving both shoulders a roll before tackling his first point. *Here we go.*

"First of all, any idiot can compile a movie list, doesn't mean they're accurate. Now, on to evidence." I raise my first finger. "The plot takes place over more than a decade. Not merely the holiday season."

Adding a second digit, I continue. "One scene that takes place on Christmas, however pivotal, does not define the genre. By that logic, *ET: The Extraterrestrial* is a Halloween movie."

"Next you're going to say *Die Hard* is not a Christmas movie."

"Completely separate debate. Also, *Die Hard* only counts as a Christmas movie if *Lethal Weapon* does."

"I'm willing to consider," he says with a casual shrug.

The nerve.

"As I was saying." I lift a third finger. "Christmas movies are *about* Christmas. Capra's film is not. It's about, among other things, a man's personal and financial struggles as he contemplates suicide."

"Yes, but it's inspirational and uplifting, which is a key element to the best Christmas movies."

I'll give him credit for trying. Some.

"True, but you wouldn't consider *Good Will Hunting* or *Remember the Titans* Christmas movies though they're similarly inspirational and uplifting. Shall I keep going?" I cross both arms before leaning a hip against Pam's desk.

"Honey, you'll save us a whole lotta time and headache if you go ahead and concede." Pam gives him a consoling pat on the forearm.

We're caught in a staring match, and I almost win until a fleck of mascara falls from the edge of my upper lashes into my left eye.

It stings! Oh, my goodness. My eye won't quit watering like someone's got the saltwater tap turned full blast. Now I'm going to have one swollen red racoon eye and one normal.

Pam earns a grateful smile with the pass of a tissue. Danger-Dan stands there, wisely remaining silent, with a look of pity on his face. *Ugh.* If there's one facial expression I can't stomach, it's pity. When my dad's philandering came to light, I saw enough to last a lifetime.

He surprises me, though, not commenting on my struggle or mega-sexy eye makeup smears. Instead, he gives me a smile bordering on affection followed by the lopsided smirk that made twelve-year-old me draw hearts and initials on the inside cover of her science notebook.

Let's forget I said that.

"I guess we'll have to watch the movie tonight and analyze it together," he announces once I've regained my composure.

"T–together?"

"Yes, Als. Together. As in, my chair beside yours while we stare at a screen and share popcorn. For discussion purposes."

He's backed me into a corner. *Must be a family trait*, I think, recalling the way his sister steamrolled me into giving him my number at the grocery store the other night. Not that he's used it.

I mean, it's not as though I've used his either, so...

What was I saying?

"I'm getting my own popcorn, Mr. Warning Label."

He smirks, and I want to smudge it off his face like an ugly shade of lipstick. "Been staring at my contact, huh? Debating whether or not to text? You don't have to overthink it. A simple 'hi' will do."

Here comes the eyeroll. I've tried hard to suppress them, I promise I have. But this man has a terrible knack for coaxing them out of me. Along with smiles, but we won't be talking about those.

"You're the worst."

"That's what my sisters have been saying for years."

"Maybe I will text you. For *their* numbers." I push off the desk and nod to Pam as I head toward my office to get back to work.

"Deal." He winks, matching my stride as he passes me a paper cup. "You might want this, though I'm guessing it's ice cold now."

"Um, thanks," I murmur, oddly touched he noticed my cocoa and thought to grab it for me when I'd completely forgotten it.

"Hi, Dan," Mrs. Mahoney's granddaughter says with a bleached white smile and a finger wave as she passes us in the hall. The girl can't be more than twenty-two, if that, and she's model-gorgeous.

Surprisingly, Danger keeps walking. Didn't he notice the slender curves and long blonde hair being tossed his direction in blatant invitation?

Huh.

Each time I think I have him figured out, he surprises and confuses me.

Which is why, when he asks about joining him for the movie tonight one more time on his way to see Silas, I find myself accepting.

Chapter 8

Dan

As far back as I remember, the first Saturday in December has been craft fair day. The annual Heights High School craft fair is the Stevens family's official holiday season opener.

"Which side are we starting with this year?" Mave yawns as we walk through the rear entrance into the cafeteria.

"Let's go left," Tory answers, nodding toward the line of tables manned by teenagers in blue polos selling breakfast burritos and doughnuts. "I see coffee."

Mave, our resident coffee addict, moans. "Where's your solidarity, huh?"

"Oh, sorry. I left it at home." Tory grins, retrieving her wallet and exchanging a few loose dollars for a tiny Styrofoam cup. "Danny might have some to spare, though."

She nods toward the farthest table with a raised eyebrow.

"No..." I groan. They can't expect me to sacrifice the one and only thing that brought me here today. I've been looking forward to this event all year with a single goal.

As a kid trying to prove his coolness, I loudly objected to Grams and Mom dragging my sisters and me out of bed early to be the first ones through the door. Sure, some of the booths had cool stuff to see, and one year I found the pocketknife that started my collection. Mostly, though, it's pottery and jewelry and crocheted goods made by older ladies who'd sell more if they paid attention to style trends. Not exactly a guy's dream Saturday.

Until the cinnamon roll lady.

Once she joined the fair, I didn't complain quite so much. They're amazing—pillowy and gooey, with exactly the right amount of cinnamon and icing. Somehow, they're not over-the-top sweet like the place in the mall.

And now two of my sisters are giving me that look—the one men cringe at, knowing we're about to sacrifice something very precious. Or there will be consequences.

"Poor Mave," Tory says, really heaping it on thick. "Can't have coffee... can't have sugar..."

Stinking gestational diabetes.

I stare longingly at the plastic wrapped rolls, round and bulging and so delicious, allowing myself a moment to consider whether it's worth the guilt trips I'm sure to receive. Four women's subtle jabs the rest of the day until I'm bleeding out like Caesar.

Correction, five women. My oldest sister, Scout, just showed up pushing her fancy three-kid stroller.

"Where's Rick?" I ask once everyone's passed around hugs and greetings to her and the munchkins.

She snorts. "Please. You won't catch him dead here."

Lucky duck.

The cinnamon roll lady meets my sad gaze with a wink. "How 'bout I bag you one to take home, sugar?"

Aye, aye, aye. Temptation.

Mave sighs. "Just eat your stupid cinnamon roll."

This smells like a trap.

"Nah, I'm good," I meet Tory's gaze with a raised eyebrow. "Unlike some siblings, *I* didn't leave my solidarity at home." See how *she* likes being thrown under the bus.

The flicker of annoyance in her steel gaze is quickly replaced with defiance and a victorious gleam. Whatever her look means, I'm not going to enjoy it. Sure enough, she leaps on me.

"Aw, still the sweetest wittle brudder ever!" Tory purses her lips into a fish face while pinching my cheeks like Great Aunt Kay did when we were little.

Mindful of the rest of the group, I give Tory a sly shove toward a nearby booth. She trips and catches herself on the edge of a rolling cart stacked with hand knit blankets. The cart topples and the thick stacks go tumbling onto the floor.

Mom gasps loudly. "*Victory Magdalene!* What on earth?"

Mom's exclamation is like old times. Tory and I were fifty-fifty for who got the blame most in our childhood scuffles. Might've been sixty-forty, since I'm Mom's precious baby boy and all. Satisfaction puts a grin on my face that's hard to smother, but I manage. Mom continues to fuss over the mess *Victory* made while apologizing to the blanket vendor.

Not one to miss an opportunity, I slip the cinnamon roll lady a ten and flash two fingers. She tucks two rolls into a white paper bag and stashes it under the table with a wink, whispering, "They'll be here for you on the way out."

"You're the best," I mouth with a discreet thumbs up.

She shakes her head and smiles, then moves on to the next customer a split second before my sisters fix their gaze on me.

"What?"

I'm the picture of innocence.

We walk as a group toward the next row of booths, Mom and Mave in the front, Tory and Scout in the middle with the stroller limousine, leaving me to walk at a more leisurely pace with Grams. It works since Mom and Mave prefer to power shop. Tory will take her time at each booth while Scout wrangles her minions. I can pretend to check stuff out while getting Grams's undivided attention.

Grams nerfs my shoulder. "I saw that." She tips her head toward the baked goods behind us.

"Can I buy your silence?"

"It'll cost you a half."

"Deal," I tell her with a grin. Knowing she loves those buns nearly as much as I do, I bought the second for her anyway.

"How are you liking the new school?"

I allow myself a moment before answering. "It's different."

"Strange having girls in your class?"

"Certainly changes the dynamic."

When I came to her struggling to choose between the all-boys' school in Texas and a public school position closer to home, Grams was the one to encourage me to venture out of state and live on my own terms.

You'll never regret the risks you take, only the ones you don't.

Her words made me brave at a time when I felt anything but.

Grams has always been able to see right through to my deepest fears and insecurities.

She was the one to encourage me to try out for track in high school, knowing I wasn't confident enough in my ball skills to go for baseball or football. Silas taught me the basics, but he injured his shoulder in Vietnam, and could only handle playing catch for so long. And while there are plenty of female athletes who throw like a boss, my sisters aren't among them. Mom would've covered me in bubble wrap if possible.

Grams understood the importance of letting boys be boys while giving me subtle lessons on what it takes to become a man who respects women. Under her watchful eye, I was never afraid to fall or to fly. I owe all of my skinned knees—both literal and metaphorical—to my grandmother.

"This is cool," I say, picking up a hand carved wooden charcuterie board. "Think Scout will use it?"

"Mm-hmm." Grams nods, playing lookout while I pay for my purchase and ask the vendor to hold on to the paper-wrapped board until we leave. "She's been on a charcuterie kick this year."

"Yeah. She'll enjoy having something to serve on that's not plastic and the kids can't destroy. Lord willing."

Grams snickers in reply.

My niece and nephews are adorable hellions. Scout does what she can to teach them to behave in public, but Rick's one of those dads who loves to rile the kids up during bedtime and turns the living room into a WrestleMania ring any chance he gets. The kids have a tough time figuring out which behavior is okay.

Take now, for example. Six-year-old Izzy has abandoned her post on the stroller's standing platform and is gushing over a booth of handmade Barbie doll outfits. Her eyes brim with tears as she begs for a white dress that has more lace and ruffles than Alessia's office last week. Meanwhile, three-year-old twins Zeke and Zack are furiously working the buckles on their seats, straining to free themselves to reach the polished rocks vendor across the aisle. The three of them make enough noise to drown out the Christmas music coming through the loudspeaker.

While Scout and Tory work to distract the kids, I race ahead of Grams to intervene. Scout will lecture me for positively reinforcing negative behavior, but I remember how hard it was being dragged around to these same booths and wanting everything I couldn't have. Or at minimum, the opportunity to explore and touch. So, I reach for my wallet once more and cough up the cash to buy Iz a doll, asking the vendor to bag the fancy white dress separately for her Christmas gift. Then I purchase two velvet pouches of polished rocks for the boys.

Once my sisters have the kids wrangled, I bribe them to stay in the stroller with my purchases. Scout narrows her eyes, but before she launches into a tirade, I gently lift a hand.

"I know. Poor behavior shouldn't be rewarded. But you deserve a little peace while you enjoy the fair, too."

Her frown melts away, and she gives me a pinched smile. "Fine. But only because I'm so tired I don't have the strength to fight you."

"How about I make it up to you? Let the kids stay at my place tonight so you and Rick can catch up on sleep." I waggle my eyebrows on the last word to restore color to her face.

"Dang, we did a good job raising you, kid." She grins, the same sideways tilt as mine. "You're on."

We eventually catch up to Mom and Mave and spend the next three hours winding up and down each hall and concourse through the massive building. I've bought gifts for two-thirds of the people on my list, including a self-care basket for my boss and a supply tote for Tory that says I'M NOT CRAZY BECAUSE I TEACH PRESCHOOL. I'M CRAZY BECAUSE I LOVE IT.

Random teacher gifts are our thing. Last year she got me a T-shirt printed with WHAT HAS TWO THUMBS AND LOVES TEACHING ENGLISH? bracketed by two cartoon hands, thumbs pointed inward. It's goofy, but I wear it regularly.

We're about to round the last hall before it circles back to the cafeteria when I spot a display of the ugliest figurines I've ever seen. Not because the artist lacks talent—quite the opposite. The figures are intentionally hideous with overexaggerated features and comical facial expressions. To the left of the booth on a set of shelves I spot a cat with an arched spine, its hair standing on end and tail straight in the air. Its eyes are bugged, and the teeth-baring snarl is classic. It's going home with me.

Now to figure out how to put it in Alessia's office where she won't immediately find it, and somehow ensure I'm there when she does, so I get to enjoy her reaction.

Or not. She might take one glance and chuck it at my head. The critter is only about four inches by two, but it's heavier than it looks. Picturing her face screwed up in outrage, it's hard not to laugh. Worth it.

I make my purchase and am still grinning to myself as I hold the door into the cafeteria open for the rest of my family. Three more people sneak through before I let go, only one murmuring thanks, but it's okay. Holding doors for people is one of the first courtesies Mom drilled into me from the time I had the strength. Right alongside saying *please* and *thank you* and *yes, ma'am.*

One more person is about to walk through from the cafeteria side when suddenly they pivot and walk briskly in the other direction.

Curious, I step through and let the door close behind me, peering after a familiar swish of dark hair. A smile creeps to my lips as Mave steps into Alessia's path.

"Alley Cat!" Mave cries, raising her arms in the air for a hug whether Alessia wants one or not.

The woman surprises me by not correcting my sister and stepping willingly into her embrace. If I'd tried that, Alessia would've fileted me like a trout.

"Nice to see you again, Maverick," she says calmly.

I know that tone. Plus, she whole-named Mave, which means she's not as happy to let the Alley Cat slide as she let on.

Once my sister releases her, Alessia glances around, eyes widening at the circle of people flanking her until her gaze lands on me. "Danger."

Mom gives me a firm nudge from behind, sending me stumbling forward much like I did to Tory earlier. I catch Tory's eye, and she discreetly mimes a tiny cat claw as she flashes a knowing smirk. Sisters are the worst.

Clearing my throat, I go for a calm, in-control greeting.

"You look pretty today," I blurt, surprising both of us.

It's the truth, but normally I'd never say so out loud. She's got her long black-brown hair down and styled the way she wore it in college. Lately when I see her at Valle, it's piled into a bun, twisted into a braid, or smoothed into a high ponytail. All of which are lovely, but I can't take my eyes off her when it's smooth and shiny like this.

Somebody pokes me in the shoulder blade, and I'm grateful for the reminder other people are here to witness my stupidity.

I clear my throat and begin introducing each of my family members, my face and neck growing hotter the longer it goes on.

We're no small clan, and she's probably itching to go on her way. Still, she's smiling and repeating each name as if committing it to memory. No doubt she's doing exactly that—at her core, Alessia cares about people.

"It's so nice to meet Danger's family," she says, her honey-brown eyes glinting with that sparkle she gets when she knows she's got the upper hand.

The T-shirt under my favorite flannel feels two sizes too small, and I have a sudden itch to beeline toward the exit. She's getting a huge glimpse into my life. While I'm proud of my family, something's happening here that makes me feel exposed.

I drag a hand through my hair, wishing I'd worn a beanie or something. Should've gotten a trim two weeks ago, but Thanksgiving was hard on Mave, so I spent my free time distracting her from missing Brian by helping her set up the nursery in my old bedroom at Mom's.

After Brian was killed, Mave couldn't stay in their apartment with the memories, and her body rebelled against climbing three flights of stairs every day. Moving home was the obvious choice. Someday she'll be ready to go out on her own again, but for now she needs family, and we're happy to be there for her with no expectations.

Everyone's gone silent. They're staring at me expectantly, but I have no idea who said what or how I'm supposed to respond.

Clearing my throat, I mumble, "Well, uh, we should probably let you go. There's a lot to see."

Tory shakes her head and mouths, "idiot."

I am, which means I need to come clean. "Sorry," I shrug sheepishly. "I spaced out. What'd I miss?"

"Maverick asked about Silas and Peggy's wedding."

Right. The supposed reason I've been spending most of my free time at Valle Encantado these days.

This might be the perfect segue into offering my family's help. She won't be able to refuse with the whole clan here, and I know they'd love to do anything to bless Silas. So much more than a neighbor, he became family.

Except this is Mave's first Christmas as a widow. We may need to tag-team to keep her distracted from the depths of grief and get enough rest for the baby. Better talk with everyone first.

"It's gonna be... interesting."

"If it doesn't kill me first. Or make us kill each other," Alessia quips.

"You're working on it together?" Mom pipes up, curiosity lacing her tone.

"Silas and Peggy asked us both to help, and as activity director, I'd be involved to some extent," Alessia explains.

"Yook, yady! Unca Dan got me wocks!" Zack bounces from the front seat of the stroller, lunging toward Alessia.

She smiles the sweetest smile I've ever seen. It sends a shock to my chest so intense I have to rub the area to make it dissipate.

"Ooh, very pretty rock. What color is it?"

"Puh-pol."

"It *is* purple! One of my favorite colors."

"I yike blue," Zack announces. I love that he hasn't mastered his Ls and Rs yet. Scout and Tory are working with him, but I secretly hope it's stubborn enough to stick around a while longer.

"Green!" Zeke argues, never one to let Zack hog the attention. "Green is gooder."

Alessia nods along as if this is a significant conversation, and I could kiss her for how sweet she's being to the boys.

Or not, with the whole *she thinks she hates me* thing.

"Hmm, I'm not sure if blue or green is better."

"She's a natural." Tory somehow manages to edge her way close enough to whisper. "You should have her come over tonight and help you babysit." She playfully gives my side a double jab with her elbow. "And after the kids go to bed, you can sort through *wedding plans*."

I shake my head at her air quotes. "Dude. Stop."

"Danny mentioned something about a theme. A movie, I think?" Grams knows the answer well and good. I griped about it at dinner the night Peggy first mentioned it. "Danger said he'd never seen it."

"To be honest, I haven't either. Which is surprising, considering I double majored in film. I've seen a *ton* of movies."

That explains a lot. Also, I can't believe I didn't know this about her.

"It's for rent on the Amazon," Grams says, her addition of *the* tugging the corners of my mouth upward. "You and Dan should watch it together. For research."

My family is going to be the death of me. How have I survived this far into adulthood without dying of mortification?

I sigh. After Maverick strongarmed Alessia into giving me her number last week, I shouldn't be surprised at Grams employing the same skills today.

At this rate, I'm going to have to dig my man card out of the industrial shredder my family's pushed it through and tape it together piece by painstaking piece.

It's Alessia's turn to surprise me, though, when she blurts, "it's not a bad idea."

Chapter 9

Alessia

I let a Stevens goad me again. How does this keep happening? I always thought I was made of stronger stuff. After all, I've been able to successfully resist Danger Stevens's charms our entire lives.

Except for that one tiny crush when I was twelve.

Seventeen. Whatever.

Two, maybe three teensy blips on the radar of the nearly two decades we've known each other.

Yet here I am, standing on his front porch at seven-thirty on a Saturday when, according to Paige, I should be on a date. If she knew whose house I was at, to watch a second movie together in as many days, there would be no end to the guffaws and insinuations. Correction: accusations and arguments to support her claims my short-lived crush never died. Paige is a future lawyer, after all.

I raise my hand to knock but scream when a voice comes from my left.

"What are your intentions toward my brother?"

"Holy Batman, Victory," I gasp, my heart thundering like a midsummer monsoon.

"Just Tory," she says, reminding me so much of her brother's *Just Dan*, I have to ask.

"Are you guys twins or what?" I nod toward the front door, then immediately want to butt my head against it. Totally stupid question since we would've been in school together too.

"Only of the Irish variety, according to Grams. He's eleven months younger."

That's right. I vaguely remember Danger—*Dan*—having a sister in the grade above us.

Tory's still talking. "Mave's three years older than me, and Scout three above her. Perfectly spaced until our little whoopsie baby Danger."

This family has the strangest names. Scout. Maverick. Victory. Danger. They remind me of those Old Testament women who saw their infant and gave them weird names saying, *"he came out of my agony"* or *"God saw my frustration."*

I should say something instead of standing here awkwardly contemplating their names and birth order. My pathetic small talk skills have all but abandoned me as I stand outside the home of the guy I've spent most of my life loathing. With his sister. Waiting to go inside and watch a movie to help us plan a theme wedding for a pair of octogenarians.

Why couldn't my brain have been in charge and said I had plans? It would've been so much easier to stream the movie at home in my pajamas with Audrey HepBun in my lap. I'm no night owl, as evidenced by my falling asleep in my chair last night while proving *It's a Wonderful Life* is not a Christmas movie in hushed whispers.

At least tonight we can talk freely without the residents shushing us.

"Are you here to watch the movie too?"

She snorts. "Definitely not. Danny would never forgive me if I messed up his first date with the infamous Alley Cat."

Her smirk kicks my pulse up a notch or ten. The second time one of his sisters has used the word *infamous* regarding me, which certainly suggests he's mentioned me. But when? Why? What has he said? Also—

"It's not a date." My palms are damp, and I feel my face reddening.

For a second, I panic, thinking she might read the old crush I for sure never had inked across my face. But that's silly. Not to mention impossible. Plus, if I did have one, it's long gone. Like, sooooo long gone. Forever ago gone. Irrelevant.

Ahem.

I am not protesting too much, Mr. Shakespeare.

"Relax, girl. I'm only teasing. It's what we do." She clips my shoulder and twists the doorknob. "Anyway, I'm only here to grab Scout's kids. They'll have more fun sleeping over at Grandma's house than Uncle Dan's, you know?"

Grabbing my hand, Tory bypasses the entire concept of knocking and instead flings the door open. She drags me inside behind her, shouting, "WHO WANTS TO GO TO GRANDMA'S FOR COOKIES?"

A chorus of cheers erupts from somewhere to the right. My gaze travels the room, taking in the dark wood paneled walls and speckled brown shag carpet. It's a weird contrast against the minimalist bookshelves (packed to the brim with books, of course) flanking the single window, sleek leather couch, and giant mounted flatscreen TV.

The space is a clash of styles that don't fit the man I know.

Then again, I don't really *know him*, know him, I suppose. But we've been acquainted for two-thirds of my life.

This is weird. *I'm* being weird.

Why did I agree to this?

I'm about to turn and leave when Danger's—*Dan's?* I can't decide what to call him anymore—head pops out from around the corner. His whole countenance brightens when he spots me standing beside his sister. Though it could be relief over the rescue she's providing. He steps fully through the doorway from what I'm assuming is the kitchen based on the apron he's wearing with flour smudges across the front.

"You made it. Give me a sec to get cleaned up and I'll send these monkeys off to Grandma's circus." He turns toward the other room making whooping noises same as my dad used to outside the Siamang enclosure whenever he took me to the Biopark Zoo.

Huh. I'd forgotten about that.

"C'mon," Tory prods me to follow. "Let's assess the damage."

We step into a kitchen fresh off a 1970s television set. I've sat through enough episodes of *Brady Bunch* and *All in the Family* with Mrs. Donato in unit 1688 over the years to know this house fits right in.

"Pardon the mess," he says, stacking bowls into the sink. "And, well, the whole house. It's a time capsule and I haven't had a chance to start the remodel yet."

There's insecurity in his eyes and tension in his smile, pricking me with guilt over being caught giving his home such a blatant onceover.

"It's old, sure, but I see the potential."

His mouth eases into a more natural smile, and my stomach flutters with an unsettling sensation—a reminder I forgot to grab dinner and nothing more. And *of course*, it growls like a mama bear guarding her cubs at the split second when everyone's quietest.

The boys break into giggles, but I'm not sure whether it was my stomach or Tory wiping their flour-covered faces that set them off.

"We made cookies!"

A little girl around the same age as my youngest half-sister proudly hoists a plastic-wrapped plate of the most hideous, misshapen cookies I've ever seen. Globs of frosting make it impossible to identify what the cutout shapes were supposed to be, but I know better than to say so within hearing range.

"Wow! Did you have so much fun?"

She responds to my enthusiastic tone with a wide-eyed head bobble. "Uncle Dan let me make 'em by myself! Well, he stirred when it got too hard 'cause of all the flour, but then I got to roll 'em and cut 'em with no help!"

"I put them in the oven," the man himself interjects.

"Well, duh," the girl says, rolling her eyes.

I'm impressed and feel an immediate affinity for this child.

"Six-year-olds can't do dang'rous things."

"So true," he nods sagely.

My cheeks ache from squashing my smile. This whole scene might cause me to burst from cuteness overload.

"Well, I hate to leave you with a mess, but..." Tory snorts. "Nope. Can't lie. I have absolutely no problem leaving you with this mess. C'mon kids, tell Uncle Dan bye!"

"Bye, Unca Dan," the twins say in unison.

"Thanks for the cookies," Tory prompts.

"Tanks for cookies," they echo, slipping into their jackets for the short walk across the street.

"Let's go, little duckies! Fly! Fly!"

All three kids follow her out of the kitchen, through the living room, and into the night with "Unca Dan" (*so cute*) and I trailing several steps behind. She boomerangs through the door to grab their bag (what's it called when they don't wear diapers anymore?) and shoots me a wink.

"Have fun, you two."

My fight against a smile is completely lost by the time she races to the front of their makeshift line, wiggling her butt and flapping her wings while getting them to mimic her duck quacks.

Tory is awesome. If the Teacher of Tiny Humans T-shirt hadn't given her away already, I'd still have her career pegged.

My host closes the door and flips the deadbolt. The action makes me feel better, strangely, because it's a habit so deeply ingrained it's unconscious. An odd action to notice, perhaps, but it's something we have in common. I've never really looked for those between me and Danger Stevens. *Dan*. I'm trying.

His head tilts to the left as though he's studying me studying him, and I feel too weird right now to do the smart thing and glance away.

"Sorry about her," he says after a long pause.

"Oh, no. I kind of love her." My laugh is awkward but honest.

"Yeah? I think she likes you, too. I know Mave does."

"Mave is hilarious. They both remind me of my sister Paige."

"How did I not know you have a sister?"

An automatic humph slips out. "Yeah, well, I didn't know about her either until I was twelve."

"How old is she?"

"Twenty-four." I wait for him to do the math knowing he and I are the same age. If I remember correctly, I'm a month older.

He plops onto the couch and motions for me to do the same. Dropping onto the cushion farthest from him, I toe off my shoes and tuck one leg up under me. Hey, if we're watching a movie, I'm going to be comfortable.

"Your folks split up when we were in mid-high, right?

"Yup."

Hopefully, he's as good a student as he was then and can read my desperate need for a subject change. My father's allergy to monogamy isn't exactly my favorite subject.

"Your dad?"

Before I formulate a response with the appropriate mix of emotions to cover my discomfort, he backtracks.

"Sorry. None of my business."

Though I've only met his family twice, it's clear they're the living-in-each-other's-pockets type. Getting in other people's business is second nature. It's no wonder he's so naturally gregarious.

Huh.

I've never considered the possibility his easy charm might be a hereditary personality trait. *Think, Alessia.* Is he funny and friendly with everyone, not only women?

It's possible. And now I know his family makeup is predominantly female, it's only reasonable he'd relate to women easily. *Ugh.* Getting to know this whole other side to Danger Stevens is throwing me for a loop.

Girl, relax.

"It's okay," I say after an inordinately long time. "And yes, Paige is my father's daughter. Well, one of them. We've lost count of how many half-siblings we have across the globe. Paige was the first one I learned about after my dad's double life came to light, when discovering I had a sister was a dream come true."

"That's wild."

"Tell me about it. He's on wife number three and I expect another pregnancy announcement any day now."

His eyes go wide. "Seriously?"

I shrug. "Wouldn't surprise me. I mean, Mom remarried about ten years ago and popped out three kids one after the other. The youngest is six. My folks married and had me right out of high school, so they're still young. Ish."

My stomach takes the moment he's processing to emit the loudest, most ungodly noise possible. My face heats, and I'd love nothing more than to sink right through the floor into the center of the earth where no one will hear that sound ever again.

"Hungry?" He chuckles, so calm and casual I could deck him.

"Brilliant deduction, Sherlock."

Violent urges and sarcasm are familiar where Danger Stevens is concerned. For the first time since arriving on his front steps, I'm in my comfort zone.

"Come on, Als, let's feed that creature before it bursts out of your belly and starts tap dancing on my counter."

I can't believe he's seen *Spaceballs*. It's a million years old, but the best movies are.

He glances over his shoulder as I'm standing there staring at him with my mouth half open and winks.

It's as if he knows he's throwing me completely off balance and allows me to regain my footing just long enough to sweep the leg like Johnny Lawrence in *Karate Kid*.

And for once, I don't completely hate him for it.

Chapter 10

Dan

"I can't believe you made these from scratch," Alessia groans, licking sauce from her fingers one by one.

"They're nothing special," I insist, but her compliments make me glad I went the extra mile. "Everything tastes better when you're hungry."

Balancing her paper plate on her lap, she reaches for another napkin from the stack on my coffee table, wiping her fingers before taking a sip of her water. She gives me a skeptical raised brow. "You battered and air-fried your own chicken tenders because they're your niece and nephews' favorite. That's the very definition of special."

She's giving me compliments and refuting my attempt to minimize. Either aliens have come and done a body swap with Alessia, or my efforts to get her to see me differently are working.

Is it possible she's softening toward me?

"Most people would grab a readymade bag from the freezer aisle and be done. But these?" She closes her eyes, touching all the tips of her fingers together in the air near her mouth. Not quite a chef's kiss but similar. "*Ottimo.*"

Now and then I catch a glimpse of her Italian side, and it makes me smile, albeit with a heavy dose of envy. I'm a basic American mutt whose only hope of understanding my roots is to send in a spit tube to one of those online DNA genealogy places. Even so, I'd only know where my ancestors came from, not their culture and traditions. It's hard not to be envious of people who have clear ties to their heritage of origin.

"Thank you," she says, moving her empty plate to the coffee table before returning to her corner of the couch. "I didn't realize how hungry I was."

"No problem. Ready?" I waggle the remote. At her nod, I click through the menus and find *Blue Hawaii.* "You know, my watched list is long, but I don't think I've ever seen one of Elvis's."

"After I watched *Jailhouse Rock* in one of my film classes, I binged a few others, but this is one I never got around to."

Elvis croons through the opening title sequence as we talk.

"I didn't know you double majored."

She shrugs. "My Nonna came from Italy not knowing more than a handful of words in English. Someone told her a great way to learn was by watching movies. When she had my dad, she used the same tactic to teach him Italian. I grew up watching her favorite old movies from both countries. Never did become a fluent Italian speaker, but I did develop an appreciation for film."

"Bet you saw your fair share of Fellini."

Alessia's smile catches me off guard. So free with everyone else, I don't think I've ever seen her give me one that wasn't full of snark or at my expense. It's stunning.

"Of course. He's not for everyone, but definitely classic."

The movie opens with one of the sexiest convertibles I've ever seen. I'm no car guy—my knowledge of classic makes and models could fill a sticky note—but even I know a beauty when I see one.

"Gorgeous," I say with a low whistle.

"She is," Alessia nods.

I grin. "I meant the car."

"So did I," she grins back.

Is it me, or did she shift an inch or two closer?

Onscreen, the airplane door opens to Elvis kissing a woman passionately as his girlfriend watches in outrage.

"Jerk," Alessia mutters, reclining toward the corner with crossed arms.

I wholeheartedly agree but say nothing. Until he tries to apologize with a song about being "almost always true" while overseas in the Army. It gets worse from there, with Elvis's character teasing the woman he purports to love in one uncomfortable move after another. A little while later, the heroine loses her top in the water, and he doesn't immediately return it.

"Is it me, or is this guy kind of a tool?"

"Thank you!" Alessia says emphatically, jutting her hand toward the screen. "Some misogyny is to be expected with this era, but *ew*. He's not much of a hero."

Elvis's character redeems himself a little when he repeatedly refuses the advances of a seventeen-year-old, until he spanks the fit-throwing teen a half hour later.

"Yeah, that scene did not age well," I say, noting Alessia's as uncomfortable as I am.

"I can't wrap my head around this being okay in any time period," she says, shifting her body toward me. "Like, who wrote this scene and said, 'you know what an emotional female needs? A *spanking*.' It's demeaning. And it happened often in movies back then. John Wayne turned Maureen O'Hara over his knee in *McLintock!* Totally ruined an otherwise great movie."

"One of Silas's favorites." While I may not have seen as many older movies as Alessia, I've definitely seen the entire catalog of John Wayne's over the years. Clint Eastwood, too. "And I agree. No man should lay a hand on a woman like that. Worse is the implication it's not only acceptable, but romantic."

Alessia props her elbow against the couch, leaning her head against her fist as she examines me as if I'm the one who's been body snatched by aliens.

"I couldn't agree more," she says after a moment.

Over the next hour, as we comment on parts we do or don't like, laugh over the more ridiculous elements and groan over others, Alessia and I somehow inch toward each other until we're nearly touching.

I'm not sure what the right call is here. Does she realize how close she is? Does this mean she's revised her opinion of me?

As much as I want to scoot another inch closer, possibly slide my arm across the back of the couch until she's tucked into my side, that's not a reality I anticipate ever happening. Not loathing me is still a far cry from welcoming my touch.

Sure, as *It's a Wonderful Life* dragged on last night, she slowly slumped toward my side until her head landed on my shoulder. But that was more about fatigue than interest. If she'd been more awake, she'd never have allowed herself to get so close, which is why I gently shifted her onto her own seat before the lights came on.

As Elvis's character sings to his bride during the final wedding scene, Alessia sighs. "This is what Ms. Peggy wants, and I have no idea how we're supposed to deliver. I mean, look." She motions to the screen. "They're standing on a flower-covered raft in the middle of a pond in Kauai, draped in leis. How are we expected to pull this off with less than a month's notice in the desert at the end of December?"

She sounds so dejected, I take a chance and slip my arm over her shoulder, drawing her into a side hug. Surprisingly, she leans into the hug and rests her head against my chest. My heart's beating the Hawaiian hula band's bongo drums.

"Want me to talk to her?"

"No," she sighs. "If this is her dream wedding, we'll have to pull it off somehow. I've been researching ideas online, but having seen her vision firsthand, I still don't know where to begin."

"Hey," I say, pulling away and waiting until she meets my gaze. "You are the most organized woman I know. You're brilliant and creative. I know you'll do everything possible to ensure Silas and Peggy have the wedding of their dreams."

"You honestly believe all that?"

The surprise in her brown eyes is killing me.

"I wouldn't say it if I didn't mean it."

She blinks several times in a row like there's something in her eyes—or she's about to cry. The way I grew up, I'm no stranger to crying jags. In all the years I've known her, though, I've never seen Alessia come close to tears. Yet, there, a single droplet escapes despite her efforts to quelch it.

With the barest touch, and slowly, because this is completely new territory for us and I don't want to mess up, I brush away the teardrop.

"You're amazing, Alessia. They're lucky to have you."

Her gaze lifts to meet mine once more, and it's torture to see the uncertainty there. She's usually so sure of herself, it's easy to forget she's capable of vulnerability too.

There's a question that's been eating at me for weeks, and I have to ask. I whisper it softly against the shell of her ear as I tighten my hold. "But who helps *you*?"

Every time I've seen her around Valle Encantado, she's hard at work. Alone, except for the brief moments I've caught her chatting with the residents or delivering coffee to Pam.

She's leaning, or maybe I am. I'm aching to throw caution to the wind and touch my lips to hers, but I can't be sure I'm reading her correctly. The last thing I want is to make the wrong move and have her decide I'm exactly the kind of guy she's always thought. If she only knew how long it's been since I've kissed a woman...

No. Better to wait until she knows for sure it's *her* I'm into, not just any female. That if—*when*, I hope—we kiss, I'll be true to her and her alone. She needs more time to know the real me.

Only, her lashes flutter closed as she lifts her chin a fraction. A clear sign she's in this with me right now.

One small kiss wouldn't—

"Sorry!"

Alessia leaps into her corner at the sound of Tory's voice. I relax against the cushion more casually than I feel.

"Izzy forgot her princess bear and won't go to sleep without it." Tory reaches behind the couch and bounces up with the pink plush I bought Iz for her first birthday. "Carry on. I didn't mean to barge in on... anything."

"You didn't!" Alessia springs off the couch. "Nothing happened. I was about to leave."

In ten seconds flat, she's got her belongings and is out the door already. Tory pauses to give me an apologetic shrug before racing across the road. I'm barely off the couch and onto my porch as Alessia backs out of my driveway.

Well, that could've gone better.

Could've gone worse, too. For the first time ever, I have hope Alessia's not as immune to me as she pretends.

Chapter 11

Alessia

Embarrassment is much easier to manage with distance and time. This is the prevailing theory I'm working with, anyway.

It's been five days since Danger Stevens wiped away my tears and lured me *this close* to a kiss. Well, that's what I think was about to happen. It's been a while.

I still cringe whenever I think about it. At this rate, our near-kiss could haunt me for two more years, which means I'll need to rely on the second half of the equation—distance.

I'd work from home if it were an option, but overseeing activities, verifying transportation, and most everything else I do for an entire community pretty much requires a hands-on approach. Thankfully, I have a storage room in desperate need of organization. Since I finished decorating the public areas for the holidays before my cocoa run on Friday, I can afford to hole up here for a few days on the off chance the confusing man tries to stop by. Bonus, the door locks automatically. So long as I have my keys, I'm happy to close myself inside and only come out to pee.

While moving boxes from their current homes and sorting through their contents, I've got a clipboard nearby in case inspiration strikes. My mind processes best when my hands are busy. Hopefully, I'll figure out a few wedding details in my head as I work.

But who helps you?

Danger lived up to his name with his question. My knee-jerk response? No one. I don't need help. Unfortunately, his question has turned itself over and under, inside out, and back again on a Möbius loop in my head ever since he whispered it.

I have no one, at least not locally, who helps with anything. And that's been fine up till now. Why should things change?

Any friendships I had in high school and college didn't stick. When enough people tell you you're "kind of *a lot*," and you're comfortable being by yourself, you don't miss the so-called friends you never really had. Besides, I get enough social interaction here at work.

Mom has Gerald and the kids. They enjoy having me around now and then, especially when they need free childcare for a night, but it's rare they reciprocate. Shortly after they were married, my car broke down. I was a college freshman living on my own (because newlyweds are not fun to live with, trust me), funded by a part-time job and no savings to speak of. I didn't have a credit card yet. You'd have thought I was asking them for an all-expenses-paid trip to the Bahamas instead of a couple hundred bucks for car repairs.

No one wants to be reminded how much they owe their parents (to the penny) for what most would consider an unavoidable necessity. I learned very quickly to tackle my own problems after that. And don't get me started on my dad.

The man has never had more than a widow's mite to spare. In fact, I remember a few times in college Dad called me from some friend's couch asking if I could Venmo him a few bucks (read: my next paycheck) to help him out till the next gig.

He's better now that he's built a reputation as a reliable studio musician, plus he signed on with the popular metal band White Hellebore a few years ago. His wife Cherise is some kind of model, so her income helps too. But with forty-two kids (five or six, whatever), it's not as though he has spare time or cash when I need him.

So, I don't. Need him, I mean. Or anyone.

Pulling out an unlabeled tub, I roll my eyes at the contents. *Nice.* Danae left an entire shelf of empty plastic tubs in here. Five containers without a single item inside. Not stacked, either. Side by side, taking up an entire shelf while the ground overflows with piles of junk. In no time, I have the bins open and am sorting and filling, allowing my mind to wander again.

Paige would be here in a heartbeat if I asked, but with law school, she can't pick up and fly here on a whim. I bought her a ticket for the twenty-third, but that's weeks from now.

Which leaves Danger. Stinking. Stevens.

I could probably text him right now and ask for his sisters' numbers, and Tory and Mave wouldn't hesitate a second before diving right in. Grams or Ms. Stevens, either. But doing so doesn't help me with my whole distance/time theory at all.

Gah! Why am I so embarrassed?

Tears are nothing to be ashamed of. They're a perfectly normal expression of emotion. Just because my father can't handle tears and my stepdad equates them with manipulation doesn't mean all men view them poorly. Dan handled them in the sweetest way possible.

The way his eyes flared with concern as he brushed my cheek so gently...

Stop! Not helping, brain.

That's it. I'm done letting my mind wander to Mr. Warning Label anymore today. There's too much to do and inspiration has yet to strike.

My checklist—precisely what I need to refocus and untangle my thoughts.

Feelings.

No, brain. *Thoughts.*

I jam the lid onto the last previously-empty bin and slide it into place on the shelf, then scan my list at the bottom of the clipboard bulleted with the requisite wedding tasks.

We'll handle the cake and meal in-house. Peggy said her daughter would take care of the invitations. Silas recruited Pastor Johns, our middle-aged chaplain—who coincidentally bears a passable resemblance to The King—to officiate. That leaves venue and décor, by far the most complicated parts of any event.

It'll be far too cold to host Silas and Peggy's wedding outdoors, but maintenance would come after me with pitchforks if I brought sand inside. I'll have to ruminate on this one.

The only venues available on the property are the common area or large dining room. If their guest list is short enough, the clubhouse attached to the indoor pool is feasible. Picturing the greenery and natural-looking boulders around the lagoon-like pool, it might be our best option.

I make a note to ask Peggy for her list right away. If I were thinking clearly the past week, I'd already have it in hand.

What's next?

A knock on the door interrupts my percolating ideas. I'd be annoyed, but frankly, I need a bathroom break and a snack.

I grab my keys and insert them into the slot on the knob. It's such an inconvenient, poor design, but my requests to change the lock have so far been met with a hard no.

"Hang on! Almost got it."

With a quick twist and push, the door swings outward fast, nearly taking out Pam and Peggy.

"Oh! I'm so sorry." With a quick yank, I free my keys and pocket them. "What's up?"

"Are you free to go over a few wedding details?"

Someday, if I'm blessed enough to marry the love of my life, I hope I'm as serenely happy as Ms. Peggy. I've heard of blushing brides and the love glow, but I don't know if I've ever actually seen it in person before her.

"Absolutely. Thanks for helping her find me, Pam."

"Of course, sugar. If you make a cocoa run later…"

A smile pulls my lips. "You got it." Motioning for Ms. Peggy to walk with me, I adjust my pace to match hers. "Let's head to my office, shall we? Wait, my list!"

Fiddling once again with my keys, I unlock the door and kick the decorative wooden wedge I use to prop it open on days I'm not in *do not disturb* mode into place. Once I have the clipboard in hand, I reverse the process and resume our walk toward my office. Ms. Peggy watches in silence with a curious tilt to her head.

"Sorry," I say. "The storage room lock is tricky. My first week, I didn't know it requires a key to open from either side and locked myself in. Took Danae two hours to find me."

"Oh dear. I imagine that was nerve wracking."

I nod in agreement, chuckling at the memory of how stupid I felt, then how desperate once my bladder began protesting.

"Especially since I left my phone on my desk."

It's one of those mistakes I laugh about now, but at the time was humiliating. Nothing says "incompetent noob" quite like locking yourself in a glorified closet without means of contacting anyone for hours. Another life lesson I learned never to repeat.

"Oh! I love it!" Peggy gushes, pointing at something ahead. "You're so clever in your decorating, Alessia!"

If it weren't the worst idea ever, I'd gladly take credit. But I can't because over the double door entry to the hallway where my office is located hangs a sprig of mistletoe.

Mistletoe is a horrible Christmas decoration. Nothing says, "hey baby, let's kiss" like a poisonous plant. And it's so cliché. I mean, how many cheesy holiday rom coms are out there coercing the main characters into a kiss to further the plot?

Some women eat that up. Me? I think it's lazy writing.

"Thank you, Ms. Peggy, but it wasn't me."

Reaching to my tiptoes, I'm able to pinch it between two fingers and pull the green bunch down. Thankfully, it's fake. I'd hate for somebody's grandchild to get ahold of the real plant and ingest it.

"Oh sweetie, leave it up. It's so romantic."

"Therein lies the problem, Ms. Peggy."

Too many Valle Encantado residents already treat me as their personal romance concierge. The last thing we need are dangling sprigs of inspiration around here. If I don't get inundated with a rash of weddings to plan, things could swing the other way and the medical staff will hold me personally responsible for the rise in STDs. I shudder to think.

The plastic plant plinks as it lands in my empty wastebasket.

"Please, have a seat." I usher Ms. Peggy into a plush guest chair, glad I was able to clear my office of last week's chaos before she came. "I'm sorry we haven't been able to connect yet this week. Do you happen to have your guest list?"

With a nod, she reaches into her pristine cream leather handbag and retrieves a folded sheet of paper. After a quick scan of her meticulous cursive, I heave a sigh of relief at the thankfully small guest list.

"I meant to ask—are you envisioning a full scene recreation for your wedding or more of an homage?"

Her answer has the power to make or break my stress levels for the rest of the year. Is it bad I wish I could be mean and tell her no way, pick something easy like *White Christmas* instead? At this point, I'd settle for any vaguely Christmasy movie instead of a Hawaiian beach one.

"First, let's see where we're at with the basics." Her request is so reasonable, I agree.

After comparing the progress made on each of our to-do lists, I feel a bit more settled. Until she makes a plea that changes everything.

Again.

"I need my son there."

"Alright..." How will this involve me?

"He refuses to come down from Santa Fe. Sara and Jillian are happy for me, but Peter considers my remarriage a betrayal of his father's memory. My husband was never comfortable at the mention of Silas. Peter's a smart boy. I'm not surprised he picked up on his father's feelings."

"I'm so sorry." My hand covers hers. "Must be quite difficult for you."

"It's not me I'm worried about," Peggy says, but her eyes are glassy with emotion. "He needs to move on. It's been ten years."

I nod, though I've never lost anyone close to me, so I can't speak to how long a person should grieve.

"But there's nothing I want more, aside from finally becoming Silas's wife, than to have my boy walk me down the aisle. Do you think..." she swallows hard, her eyes pleading.

My stomach already knows what she's going to ask before she finishes her sentence. It's flipping and flapping like a spastic fish lives in there.

"Do you think you could go and persuade him to come? Please? I sold my car after my eyes got too bad to drive at night, and it's hard on these old bones being in the car so long."

I'm going to regret this. "Of course, I'll go."

She sighs with a grateful smile. "Bless you, sweet girl. Oh, I'll feel so much better knowing Dan has company!"

Um, what?

"Dan?"

"Oh yes," she nods emphatically. "He's got a nice SUV that'll be safe in the winter weather."

Winter weather. *Right.* It's the desert. We'll be lucky to see any real weather before February. I can count on one hand the number of white Christmases I've seen in Albuquerque in my lifetime.

"Besides, I'm not sure Peter will agree to see Dan. But he's a... what's the term they use now? *Girl dad.* You remind me of my granddaughters. I know he'll hear you out."

So much for my distance/time theory.

Half a day or more trapped in an SUV on the road with Danger Stevens. Doesn't sound like a recipe for trouble at all.

Chapter 12

Dan

"You want me to go where?" I heard them the first time; I just don't understand why. "What's in Santa Fe?"

Ms. Peggy launches into a literal sob story about needing her son to walk her down the aisle and her wedding will be ruined if he doesn't agree to come. For some reason this can't be accomplished by phone. It must be done in person.

Unlike their current ask, which is happening on my lunch break via FaceTime. Why did I have to teach Silas how to use his "newfangled iPhone thingy"?

Ms. Peggy sniffles, wiping her eyes with a tissue Silas handed her from offscreen. I can't refuse a woman who reminds me of a sweeter version of Grams when she's crying buckets over her baby boy. It hits far too close to home. My conscience prods with *what would I want someone to do for Mom or Grams if they were this desperate?*

"All right," I concede on a long exhale.

Guess I'm going to Santa Fe on Friday afternoon.

"Got a bead on an Elvis suit for Pastor Johns," Silas adds, his face coming into view as Peggy hands off the device. "An old buddy who was a Vegas impersonator. Easy to pick up while you're there."

The speaker crackles in my ear as Silas fumbles to disconnect the call. I crack my neck side to side to release the tension before scarfing the rest of my sandwich. My next class is in five minutes. I should be shifting gears to AP Lit, but my mind's still on Santa Fe.

Ms. Peggy doesn't drive anymore, but Silas still drives his beat up 1986 Ford F-150 Lariat on the rare occasions he leaves Valle Encantado. Since I taught him how to order groceries online a few years ago, he doesn't go anywhere, except to hang out with his Vietnam buddies at the VFW and the occasional checkup Valle's services don't cover. Santa Fe's a long distance for him, though, so it's no real surprise the out-of-town job's been delegated to me.

I'm not mad about it, especially since Alessia hasn't needed my help with anything so far. To be honest, I think she's avoiding me. After arguing with myself for too long, I broke down and texted her a few days ago to clear the air after our movie night. She didn't respond, and I can't say I'm not disappointed.

I thought we'd had a *moment*.

Not a term most men would use, I know. But thanks to the number of chick flicks I've been forced to watch due to the overabundance of females in my life, I know a *moment* when I'm in one.

My guess is she'll use her own capability (read: inability to accept help) to keep her distance for a while. She doesn't need to reply for me to get the message. I'm not her type, and she's not interested in getting to know me after the glimpse she got last weekend. Got it.

Am I disappointed? Of course.

I've liked Alessia since sixth grade social studies when I returned to school after a bad case of the flu, and she'd made me a hand-copied set of the notes I'd missed. For the rest of the year, I noticed her kindness and attention to detail with other people too. Plus, even then, she was beautiful with those big eyes and long, dark hair.

She never quite fit in with any one crowd, but I admired how she didn't strive to fit in like the rest of us. I'd thought we were friends, but something happened that year, and she started acting as if my existence was a personal affront.

In high school, her digs and eyerolling kicked into high gear. That's when I made a game of pushing her buttons and calling her Alley Cat. Even if she didn't want to be friends or date me like the other girls did, I craved her attention.

We're not twelve anymore. If she genuinely wants nothing to do with me, I'll have to get over my disappointment and move on.

Still, I can help her from the sidelines. If tackling this one task for Ms. Peggy and Silas's wedding will check another item off what I'm sure is a mile-long to-do list for Alessia, I'm in.

It's not ideal, but if I run home and change after work Friday, I'll be in Santa Fe before two. An hour's drive, another two to chat up Ms. Peggy's son and secure the Elvis costume, then an hour home puts me back in town by dinnertime.

Not like I had anything better to do except crash the next community Christmas movie with Silas.

I really ought to reconnect with friends my own age.

Not here at work, though. One takeaway from my time in Texas I won't soon forget—work relationships are the surest path to finding yourself out of a job.

Turning my 4Runner into the Valle Encantado parking lot at 1:55p.m. on Friday, I quickly locate a space and jog to Silas's apartment, waving to Pam as I pass the front desk. I got stuck in a last-minute parent-teacher conference that ran long, but Silas asked me to stop by and pick something up before heading out of town. A delivery to another "old buddy" while I'm conveniently already there, I'm sure.

Silas opens the door with a crooked cat-got-the-canary grin resembling a few of his old movie heroes and one of mine, Mr. Harrison Ford.

"How are the twerps?" he asks.

Oh, I'm supposed to let his sneaky grin slide? And what's with the boyish heel-bounce?

"They're fine. Finished Hemingway, now I get to torture them with grammar for the next week till finals."

"Don't you teach something else on Fridays?"

He knows full well Fridays are for the kids' electives, which is why we dismiss early. As one of the few bookish teachers at a STEM school, the admins recruited me to head up the creative writing and yearbook classes. The other four weekdays are long and intense with college-preparatory classes.

"Silas," I say in my most authoritative educator voice. "What's going on?" There's something fishy here, and I aim to figure out what.

"Nothin'," he shrugs casually. *Too* casually.

"Uh huh. Then what's with the self-satisfied grin, huh? It's the same one you get after messing with telemarketers."

He chuckles. "Hey, if they don't want to be toyed with, they shouldn't be toying with innocent folks in the middle of dinner."

"Innocent. Right."

Silas claps a hand to the edge of my shoulder. "You know me too well, son. Keep your shorts on, Peggy's almost here, and then you can head out."

I'm itching to correct his idiom from *shorts* to the proper *shirt*, but I have a feeling he'd explain why his version works better. And with Silas, he'll make the explanation as inappropriate as possible just to watch me squirm.

"What am I picking up exactly? Is it a delivery or another errand?"

"Like I said, keep your shorts on."

Motioning toward my dark wash jeans, I retort, "Fully dressed, as you can see."

Silas shakes his head, then jolts as someone taps on his door three times in rapid succession. His face breaks into the smile he reserves for Peggy as he flings the door wide.

"Right on time," he says, leaning to press a kiss to the top of his fiancée's head.

The diminutive woman isn't alone. My heartrate kicks up as Alessia plants herself in the doorway, the stiffness in her body language communicating an inability to choose between coming inside or fleeing. My money's on fleeing, so when she takes a hesitant step through the door, I'm happily surprised.

"Are you ready?" Her tone is flat, face expressionless as she crosses both arms and heaves a loud, impatient sigh.

Ah. We're back to this again. So much for progress.

Then my ears flag on what she said. "Ready?"

"To hit the road?" There goes the classic Alessia Catano eyeroll. "If we leave now, we'll be back in time for *Miracle on 34th Street*."

"We?" I'm an intelligent man most of the time, I swear.

"Santa Fe?" she says, rolling her hand in front of her as she drags out the words in a tone typically reserved for the most clueless of morons.

It's me. I'm the moron.

That's when I notice she's not sporting her usual khakis and Valle Encantado polo. Her hair's piled on her head in one of those intentionally messy buns women wear that look like they threw it up in seconds but really took fifteen minutes to perfect. She's wearing a loose button-down with the front casually tucked into a pair of relaxed button-fly jeans that make her legs look a mile long, and a soft leather bag hangs from one arm with a wool coat draped over the top.

What's the expression Silas used when he saw Peggy for the first time after sixty years? Right—she's knocked me sideways.

Dislodging my tongue from its trek down my throat, I thumb toward the guest bathroom. "Uh, yeah. Gimme a sec."

Alessia looks so pretty, I wonder if she had a date planned for later. I grit my teeth against the image of her smiling freely with someone else after the one she gave me last weekend felt like such a reward. Jealousy sours in my gut, but then I remind myself she can't go on a date if we're in Santa Fe.

A wicked gleam and Harrison Ford-like grin of my own reflects in the mirror as I wash up. Before I go, I give myself a quick onceover. With any luck, I'll persuade Alessia to join me for dinner, and she won't be embarrassed to be seen with me in an untucked white tee under an open flannel shirt.

Funnily enough, we almost match with the thin lines of my flannel in the same yellow gold as her coat. For once I'm glad a parent kept me late, so I didn't have time to change into the thermal Henley and joggers I intended to wear on the road.

Since no one warned me about Alessia. Intentional? Knowing Silas and Peggy, absolutely.

"That everything?" I ask the devious duo as I return to the living room.

"Here are the addresses," Peggy says, slipping me a sheet of stationery edged with purple flowers, her precise handwriting in neat lines across the middle.

Alessia swipes the sheet from between my fingers. "You drive, I'll navigate."

"Yes, ma'am."

Silas and Peggy wear matching smirks as I spin my keys around one finger and hold the door for Alessia.

"I know what y'all are up to," I murmur before ducking out the door, pointing two fingers at my eyes and then at them.

Every nerve vibrates with anticipation as Alessia and I stride in sync past the front desk and into the parking lot, but I'm trying to play it cool.

Stuck in my SUV with no one else available, she won't be able to avoid talking to me. This could be my only chance to smooth over whatever went wrong Saturday night and regain the footing I somehow lost. Or accept defeat and let her go.

I can't blow it.

She's smart, though, and we have a long history of her assumptions getting in the way. I'll have to pivot and try to counteract her animosity without my reliable arsenal of humor and charm, since those are the qualities that set her off most.

Now to figure out how.

Chapter 13

Alessia

"No way *Gremlins* is a Christmas movie!"

I cross my arms and lean against the door, avoiding the nauseating streak of motion out the windows of Danger's 4Runner as we speed along I-25 near Bernalillo. We returned to our debate from last week with gusto the second our butts hit the seats twenty minutes ago.

He started it.

I *will* finish it. And win.

"Please," he scoffs. "You conceded to the *Die Hard* and *Lethal Weapon* debate. How is *Gremlins* different?"

"It just is!" I'm drawing a blank on the many reasons he's wrong, but I know he is.

While my brain skips around like a hopscotch champion, my road trip companion remains blessedly silent for the next five minutes as Christmas carols play over the radio. His 4Runner predates Bluetooth connectivity, so we're stuck with the 24/7

Christmas radio station. Somebody somewhere is going to hate me for saying this, but if I have to listen to Mariah Carey shriek about what she wants for Christmas one more time, I'm going to stab my eardrums with one of the five thousand straws in Dan's glovebox.

I said what I said.

Whitney Houston's (the *real* queen, if you ask me) soulful rendition of "I'll Be Home for Christmas" comes on, which sparks another topic in my memory. Debating with this man might be my new favorite pastime.

"Okay, you said Grams was a huge Cary Grant fan—" From the driver's seat, he confirms with an "mm-hmm," and my heart skips a beat because who would've thought Danger Stevens was the kind of guy to sit and watch old movies with his grandmother? "So, I assume you've seen *The Bishop's Wife*?" At his nod, I continue. "How about the 1996 Denzel and Whitney remake, *The Preacher's Wife*?"

"I've seen both."

"Which is better?" Yes, I asked more smugly than a girl who is undecided probably should, but I'm curious whether he has an opinion I can contradict merely on principle.

It's pathetic how much I enjoy sparring with this man.

He glances at me briefly, then returns his focus to the road shaking his head and grinning.

"What? It's a good question."

"An unanswerable one."

"It's perfectly answerable. Now choose."

"Oh no," he's shaking his head. "I am not going to say Denzel simply to have you spend the next thirty minutes enumerating the ways Cary made the better angel. Or vice versa, as the case may be."

Oh, he's good. I'll give him that. He's giving me absolutely nothing to work with. But it's not as if I can let go and, what, talk about normal subjects? Civilly? We've never done that before.

After a brief back-and-forth which ends in a stalemate, the conversation switches to the countless iterations of Charles

Dickens's *A Christmas Carol*. Ever the English teacher, Dan retorts with the inevitable "the book was better."

"Of course, you'd say that." My eyes roll as predictably as his argument. "I wouldn't know."

His slack-jawed expression is priceless. "Never?"

"I haven't read a single work of fiction since college, and even then, not by choice."

The man makes a show of rubbing his chest. "That hurts. You've caused me actual pain, Alley Cat."

I can't help it. My laughter fills the cab.

He glances at me dumbstruck before refixing his gaze through the windshield. The tension ratchets up as the silence drags on.

I'm out of Christmas movies at this point *(gasp!)*, but I've been enjoying the easy flow of conversation in what I'd worried would be a tense car ride. I'm not ready for it to end. So...

What do we talk about now?

My life isn't exactly exciting. Other than work, chatting with Paige, and hanging out with my rabbit, I don't do much.

I already overshared about my weird relationship with my parents. A huge leap for me. I don't typically talk about my family. Or anything else uncomfortable, really, except with Audrey. She's been my only real sounding board since I quit seeing my therapist years ago.

Even my conversations with Paige only go so deep.

I could sneak in a short nap like I used to as a kid when we'd venture into Santa Fe or Taos to play hometown tourist between Dad's touring gigs. Except that would be rude. Plus, I'm not sure how I feel about Danger Stevens watching me sleep. What if I drool or snore? (Also, why is the habit of full-naming him so hard to break?)

My mind blanks the harder I try to think of a conversation topic, but I eventually land on something.

"You spent a few years in Texas, right?"

He mentioned as much the other night as he reheated those incredibly craveable chicken tenders while I watched in drooling awe. I've never been one to freak out about a man who cooks. It's not as if gender influences one's ability to prepare food. But there is something vulnerable, intimate, and oh-so-appealing about one person offering another tasty sustenance made with their own two hands.

Goosebumps break out along my arms at the memory.

Also, I'm getting hungry.

"Cold?" He reaches for the temperature controls on the dash.

"A little." White lies aren't actual lies, are they?

I notice he hasn't acknowledged my question. "Texas?"

He drags in a long, slow breath, the kind I do when I need a minute to calm and refocus my tangled thoughts.

"Yeah."

"Teaching?"

He nods. "Spent half a dozen years teaching at an all-boys private school."

There's satisfaction and pride in his tone. I don't know why I always pictured him teaching in some *Dangerous Minds* sort of situation. *Dead Poets Society* fits him so much better.

My cheeks flush at the idea of him as Mr. Stevens, the kind of laidback yet impassioned teacher who inspires his students to stand on their desks and sneak out into the night to recite poetry. It's pathetic how easily the image forms in my mind's eye, more so how my heart skips a beat.

Warning lights go off inside my head.

This is neither the time nor the place to resurrect old crushes.

Focus, Alessia.

"What brought you home?"

Danger works his jaw a long minute. The knuckles of his left hand go white on the steering wheel as he stares unblinking ahead. Each passing second brings my nerves closer to a fever pitch. Whatever the reason, it must be bad. No one waits this long unless it's painful, right?

"Mave's husband was killed in June."

My stomach sinks. Emotion floods my system, overwhelming me with waves of feeling.

Mom used to shake her head in frustration at how I'm either completely closed off or achingly empathetic. There's precious little middle ground. Right now, I'm awash with grief for a man I know nothing about on behalf of a woman I've met twice. And for the upheaval such a loss must have cost the man beside me.

What happened? Is Mave okay? From looking at her, you'd never know she was a recent widow... though now that I think about it, there *has* a been a shadow in her eyes that doesn't fully dissipate when she smiles.

This man moved home for her. *Wow.*

So many questions, but only one is safe to ask.

"You gave up a job and a life you must've loved to be here for your sister?"

Danger never fails to surprise me. I mean, who does that—upend their entire life for their family? My dad would never. Mom either. Paige might, but would I?

No, I can't say I would. Not even for Paige. Sure, I'd show up on her doorstep at the first sign she needed me and stay until I knew she was okay, but give up my job and move...

That's major.

"She needed her family," he shrugs. "Besides, it wasn't much of a sacrifice. Things in Texas were... complicated."

The fingers of his right hand tap a rapid beat on his knee while the rest of his body sits rigid and tense. He reaches out to fiddle with the heater again, then the stereo. My eyes narrow as I continue to study the man beside me from the comfort of my little corner. I've got one knee bent with my foot on the seat. It's comfortable, but my casual position is a tactical move as well.

The vibes he's putting off are intense. I feel them the same way I experienced such grief a few minutes ago. If I appear comfortable, he might relax, otherwise he'll perceive my questions as a threat. (At least, that's how *my* brain works.)

I have *so* many questions.

His fidgeting is starting to get to me by the time he speaks. "So, uh, how'd you become an activities director?"

His subject change throws me off balance.

We've come a long way in the last few weeks, but a handful of light conversations about movies and our families aren't in the same realm as the soul-baring discussion his level of discomfort implies. So, as desperately as I want to know what happened to Mave's husband and the real reason he left Texas, letting it slide for now is clearly what he needs.

Instead, I tell him about Nonno and how lost he was after Nonna died. How Dad had to put him in a nursing home, and the way it broke my heart to see my precious grandfather waste away between visits.

"He started spending time with a few of the other residents on his better days. I noticed how much more vibrant he was on days they had something to do besides watch television while waiting to die." I drop my left foot onto the floorboard and lift my right instead. An hour doesn't seem like a long car ride, but my tush starts to go dead around the forty-minute mark. "Which is morbid, I know. But realistic."

He gives one of those *you're not wrong* kind of shrugs. I have to say, it's nice being on the same side of something for once.

"Anyway, around the same time, I realized I'd rather watch movies than make them. But I'm not a great writer, so becoming a critic is out, and a girl's got to eat and pay rent somehow."

His soft chuckle warms me through. "How'd you wind up at Valle Encantado instead of your nonno's nursing home?"

Sadness burns in my eyes as it always does when I think about my grandpa too long.

"He passed away my third semester."

"What's your favorite memory with him?" Danger asks, surprising me yet again with his sensitivity.

Dan. Not Danger. He's trying, so should I.

For the next fifteen minutes, I share my favorite Nonno and Nonna stories. He laughs in the right places, and each time the sound fills me with warmth and light. By the time we arrive at Peter James's single-story adobe home on the outskirts of northern Santa Fe, I become aware of two sensations at once: my arms ache to wrap around Dan and soak up as much of that warmth and light as possible, and I desperately need a bathroom break.

He opens the door, jolting me from my stupor. More like pulling me, since my mind feels as rubbery and stretchy as taffy on a puller machine. My gaze meets his, and I add lungs to the list of parts functioning poorly today.

I can't be fantasizing about how it would feel to hug *Danger Stevens*. I'm still off balance after our moment in his house with that near-kiss we haven't talked about.

What is happening to me?

And why am I hoping it keeps happening?

Chapter 14

Dan

Alessia has a knack with people, and it's beautiful to behold.

Peter James could've given Ebenezer Scrooge a run for his money when he first opened the door, but in no time at all, she had him sending a boy off to procure a turkey for Bob Cratchit and Tiny Tim. Except the boy was me, and I procured burritos.

By the time we finished our insanely early dinner, she'd convinced Ms. Peggy's son to not only come to the wedding but walk his mother down the aisle. I was there, yet I couldn't tell you how she managed it.

That's not the craziest part.

Getting to the Elvis impersonator guy's house was tricky. The GPS kept taking us through nonsensical twists and turns ending in front of a tattoo parlor a few blocks off the historic Plaza. Alessia and I devolved far too quickly into bickering, but before I had a chance to prove to her men sometimes *do* ask for directions, we were interrupted by a knuckle rap on her window. She eased it open an inch at the sight of a massive, burly dude with the wickedest beard I've ever seen.

Me? I would've reversed out of the place faster than you can say "gauged ears," but Alessia simply smiled at the man and said, "I think we're lost."

The softspoken man melted into heart eyes (which, dude, I get it) and found the problem in two seconds. I had clicked the street name with *drive* instead of *avenue* on the nav. Luckily, the correct address was only a few blocks away, and thanks to Alessia's knack, we got pulled into a lively conversation with Silas's friend Terrance for forty-five minutes before leaving with one white sequined jumpsuit in hand.

"Tell Silas we're even," the old man chuckled before closing his front door.

Alessia is quiet now that our errands are complete. Resting her head between the window and the headrest, her eyes are closed with a tiny V etched between her brows as she focuses on her breaths. In for three, out for four. I've noted this about her over the years—when she's on, she's *on,* but as soon as no one's looking, it's like her depleted battery requires a full retreat to recharge.

Some might perceive her as an extrovert with how she engages people in conversation and the effortless way she smiles, treating everyone as old friends. The fact she struggles to be this way around me is part of why I've always been so drawn to her. She doesn't conceal her grumpiness or sass, doesn't fake a smile to be nice when she doesn't want to. Alessia is completely herself when I'm around, and I'm honored.

I don't know why she lets me see her in full introvert recovery mode. Could be the same reason she never bothered to hide her disdain and freely expressed her displeasure for my interactions with other women—she never sought to impress me, never considered me a viable option romantically. This might put off any other man, but with the teasing way my family expresses their love, the back-and-forth between me and Alessia has always felt like a form of affection.

Her silent meditation stretches as I navigate the darkening streets lit by streetlamps and the faintest traces of sunlight reflected in the clouds along the horizon. Our errands are complete, bringing this strange and brief road trip to a close, but I'm not ready to go home. I still need to learn why she raised her walls after our moment last week. Lord knows I've tried to give her space, but I don't want to go back to how we were.

Traffic's getting tighter the closer we get to the Plaza. Traffic equals people, which is the opposite of what she needs right now.

"Als?" I glance toward the passenger seat, gently shaking her knee.

Her eyes blink open. "Where are we? I thought we were going home."

"Can you check your phone to see what's happening at the Plaza? Thought it might be fun to walk around and grab dessert before we head home, but it looks like there's an event."

Her frown deepens, but she unlocks her phone, fingers tapping away at the screen. The light at the next intersection turns red, and I brake to stop behind a blue minivan.

"Tonight is Las Posadas." There's a wistfulness in her tone that sparks hope she's willing to spend more time with me.

"I've always heard about it, but never been. Have you?"

She shakes her head, dragging her lower lip between her teeth as her gaze bounces over the buildings and pedestrians outside her window.

"We weave through this traffic, hit the interstate, and we'll be home in an hour."

Alessia doesn't answer, and the light changes to green. With another quick glance before I press the gas pedal, I glimpse the indecision in her eyes.

"Or... we can find a place to park and check it out. Grams used to tell stories about it. A couple dressed as Mary and Joseph travel around the Plaza seeking accommodation but are heckled by the devil as each innkeeper refuses them lodging."

"Yeah, I've heard the same, but never made the time."

A lifted truck pulls away from the curb ahead leaving ample space. I grin, ready to flex my parallel parking skills at the first sign she wants to stay.

"I don't have any plans tonight," I venture before considering she may have a Friday night event at the community to oversee. Or date. "Do you need to get home?"

"No, Pam said she'd manage movie night."

I jut my chin toward the space ahead, praying we'll get there before someone else takes it. "Stay?"

"Yeah." She nods with a hint of a smile at the corners of her mouth. "Let's play tourist."

My own lips curve into a grin. I was hoping she'd say that.

"*Four* tries!" Alessia guffaws, slapping her thigh and wheezing with poorly suppressed laughter as I join her on the curb.

My injured ego has me frowning, but the frown's more playful than I feel because it's hard to be irritated when she's this amused. I love the way her hair cascades behind her as she throws her head back in laughter.

"It's not *that* funny."

She raises one eyebrow, lips twitching. "Oh, but it is."

"I'm normally excellent at parallel parking."

"I believe you." She nods solemnly, then snorts at her own straight-faced lie as she ropes a thick scarf around her neck with nimble gloved fingers.

My face and neck are blazing with embarrassment, but that's what I get for telling her, "I got this," like a cocky nitwit and then completely misjudging my angle when she smiled. The second time, I managed to avoid looking at her as I pulled forward, lined myself up, backed in... and hopped the curb.

Performance anxiety is a thing, okay? I'm not proud of it, but I am man enough to admit I messed up. Three times.

I'm never living this down. Alessia won't let me. Guaranteed.

"Can we go, please?" I huff.

"Ooh, somebody's testy," she says pushing her lips out in a funny grumpy-baby voice as she pokes my bicep.

Fighting a smile, I give her the stink eye before placing my palm to her lower back and guiding her around to my left so I'm on the street side. "No, I just made a fool of myself."

She bumps into me too hard to be accidental. Glancing down, my pulse stutters at the beautiful smile on her face. Not teasing or pitying, it's an honest smile filled with affection and humor that steals my breath. It's the kind of smile that would tempt me to drag her into an adjacent alleyway and press her against the wall as I dive in for the kiss of our lives… if I didn't think it would result in a swift knee to the groin.

"If I tell you an embarrassing secret, will it help you feel better?" Her softspoken words curl white into the chilly night air.

"Absolutely."

It won't, but I'm not about to miss the chance to learn something she wouldn't ordinarily admit to.

"I can't parallel park at all. It would've taken me way more than four tries plus extensive damage to the vehicles in front and behind."

Impulse overtakes me as I spin her away from oncoming foot traffic into the alcove of the nearest doorway and sweep her into a tight hug. Pressing a kiss to her temple, I set her on her feet before touching my forehead to hers.

She's stiff as a board in my arms, so I release her awkwardly, humiliation cascading over me fresh and hot.

"I'm sorry," I choke out. "Don't know why I did that."

Alessia closes the distance I put between us and wraps her arms around my middle, pressing her cheek to my chest.

I don't know what to do with this. Aside from the comforting side-hug I gave her last week, we've never hugged before. She's certainly never initiated contact. Tentatively, I let my arms enfold her once more. No way she doesn't feel the pounding of my heart against her ear.

My mouth is full of the words I've wanted to tell her for ages. How much I like her, how I will treat her the way she deserves, what her smile does to my insides. Before I get the chance, her arms drop to her sides, and I'm forced to let her go.

The fragrance of oranges tickles my nose as she steps backward and resumes walking toward the Plaza. My brain's absolute mush as I turn to catch up, once again putting myself between her and the street despite the thickening crowds spilling over into the streets.

I should say something. Clear the air.

"Magical," she says in an awed whisper as we approach the Palace of the Governors.

"Mm-hmm," I agree, and the mood between us shifts.

A large lit Christmas tree glows from the middle of the Plaza. Mature trees are strung with white and colored lights, and electric luminarias line each tier of the surrounding buildings. Santa Feans call them *farolitos*, but the terms are interchangeable, and a sight unlike anywhere else.

Each time I'm in Santa Fe, I'm reminded of why it's called "The City Different." With a blend of cultures and history from the 1600s, each visit is a new experience. It's clear from the throngs of people this is a bit of local tradition that goes back decades or longer. A multitude of people line the street across from the Palace of the Governors, an ancient adobe building and the anchor of the Plaza.

Alessia reaches for my hand. I glance down in surprise, meeting her gaze in the warm glow of light. She shrugs with a nonchalant smile. "I don't want to lose you."

She means in the crowd, but the sappy part of me hears what it wants.

I squeeze her gloved hand and tug her toward a bundled-up volunteer distributing white candles with cardstock disks around the base. Somebody tips their flame onto Alessia's wick. It catches, and she tilts hers to light mine. I spot the pair representing Mary and Joseph ahead to the right, and a crowd behind them begins to follow.

Those at the front of the line carry large lit candles in hurricane glass mounted as torches. Behind them, musicians pluck their guitars. Oddly enough, there's a violinist in the mix. Someone begins singing along in Spanish, and soon after much of the crowd joins in. The procession walks past us, picking up in size, before coming to a stop in front of an "inn." Someone knocks loudly, then a booming voice cries out in Spanish.

Alessia leans toward me and asks, "Do you know what they're saying?"

I shake my head. Spanish would've been more practical, but I took French in school because the girls were cuter.

An older man in a brown coat and cowboy hat pipes up from behind us with a heavy Spanish accent. "*Posada* means inn. They're asking for a room at the inn. Look up."

Our gazes follow his outstretched hand to a man dressed in biblical-style garb standing outside on the second level behind a row of farolitos, arms crossed with a frown on his face. He shouts harshly, waving his arm in the air.

The older man translates again. "The innkeeper says to go away, there is no room here."

"Thank you," Alessia tells the man, gifting him with her smile.

His eyes crinkle with a return smile, though his mouth is hidden behind the thickest, most amazing mustache I've ever seen. My hand runs along the beard I've maintained since No-Shave November.

The crowd boos. The innkeeper repeats his declaration, and the throng follows Mary and Joseph to the next "inn," where the scene is repeated. This happens a few more times until everyone returns to the Plaza center. After cider and cookies, the crowd thins, though a considerable number linger around the gazebo.

"Ready to head home?" I ask, missing the warmth of Alessia's hand, which I had to release so she could hold her Styrofoam cup of cider.

A band plays the intro to "Silent Night" from inside the gazebo. All around, the crowd begins to sing along.

"I know the words to these. Let's stay and sing."

We find a spot in the crowd and join in on the next stanza of "Joy to the World." It's one of the few carols I know the verses to, so I let loose. I did a few years of choir in high school, and occasionally sing backup with the worship team at church. So, unlike my parking job earlier, my singing skills won't embarrass me in front of Alessia.

It takes another song for the crowd to warm up, but everyone mostly sounds pleasant. Except for one truly horrendous voice coming from my left. The poor lady sounds like a goose gagging on a kazoo.

Oh no. It can't be.

But it is.

Alessia's singing along for all she's worth. Loud, with a passion that would be admirable if it weren't so painful.

I wince as the band flows into "O Holy Night," easily the most butchered song in the entire holiday music repertoire, and it's as bad as I feared. As in, she's trying to hit the last high *divine* with delusions of Celine Dion while everyone in a fifteen-foot radius steals wide-eyed glances.

I'm never going to hear the beloved song the same again.

After this, I may never hear *at all*.

The song ends, and the assembly disperses as the band packs away their instruments. The murmurs from a few people nearby aren't exactly kind, so I hope Alessia remains oblivious to whom they're murmuring about. She catches me frowning after them and puts a hand on my forearm as though she's worried I'll give them a piece of my mind. Which I would if I weren't more interested in protecting her ignorance.

"I know they're grumbling about my horrible singing voice. It's okay." Her brown eyes glisten above flushed pink cheeks as she smiles. "It's the worst, or so I've been told. Mrs. Cranston banned me from helping with the holiday choir and Senior Sing-a-Longs years ago, so now I only sing when I can get lost in the crowd."

She has no idea that voice could never be lost unless the crowd were in the aviary of the zoo. But I'm not about to tell her so. Not with how she's looking at me.

"The psalmist said to 'make a joyful noise,' right?" She grins, bouncing on her toes with her nose pink from the cold and looking so completely adorable I might risk the knee to the groin and kiss her. "There's no sweeter worship music than Christmas carols in my book."

"You're a believer?" I ask, breathless, because if her answer is yes, she's no longer merely a crush. She's my perfect woman.

She nods, her eyes rounding as she asks, "You too?"

I'm done for.

Now to convince her I'm her perfect man.

Chapter 15

Alessia

"I'm in trouble," I tell Paige after church on Sunday as I attempt to hold a squirming Audrey HepBun.

Audrey's natural flight instincts are kicking in since I'm a ball of tension. With my emotions in such a jumble, all I wanted was to cuddle my bunny, focusing on the softness of her fur against my hand in hopes it would help settle my mind. Instead, I'm upsetting her. *Sigh*.

I set her free on the small patch of grass and adjust my grip on the phone pressed to my ear. Audrey glares at me, thumping her foot loudly against the ground in displeasure before hopping away. If I weren't so stressed, I'd laugh.

"What's wrong? Should I come early? What do you need?" Paige pelts me with questions, her own natural instincts taking over for a sister in need.

After a swig of lukewarm cocoa, I inhale deeply and assure her I'm fine. "No, I'm being overdramatic."

"You? *Never*."

"Rude," I say, suppressing a laugh. "It's nothing life-threatening, okay? Just potentially earth shattering. For me."

"Spill," she commands. "Everything. Is this about that guy?"

Danger Stevens may have been the subject of more than a few calls the past month or so. Still, this is a big step for me. If I tell Paige, then my feelings become real.

"*Les*," she says. "You called me, now spill."

"Objection. Badgering," I retort.

"Overruled."

"Fine. I..."

Why is this so hard to say? I've been thinking the words on a loop ever since the drive home from Santa Fe the other night.

"I maybe... like him."

Once we found the 4Runner and I harassed him one last time about his parking job, we talked nonstop the whole ride home in the warmth of the heater and our shared experiences. We skirted the serious topics, but the conversation was no less meaningful. I never imagined we'd have so much in common.

And ever since, I've had these crazy feelings.

Only since then?

Shush, brain. That's my story, and I'm sticking to it.

Paige squeals. "Like him? As in, no longer want to claw his face off, or you're considering kissing his face off?"

For the love.

"Um, is there an option in-between?" While I'm not adverse to the latter *someday*, it's a skosh faster than I'm ready for.

No one has ever accused me of being a fast mover when it comes to relationships. A third date would be moving faster than I historically go. Most guys tend to show their true colors a few minutes into the first date, and the rest by date two. I've yet to date a man who's been able to ignore anyone else with boobs while on a date with me. Is it too much to ask a guy to control his gaze and not return flirty smiles from other women?

Call me crazy, but I think that's a pretty low bar.

"Sure," Paige answers. "You could ask him out."

I scoff. She chuckles.

"You could 'accidentally' get stuck in the storage room."

"I should have known you'd use my fear against me."

She laughs. I don't.

"I'm serious, Paige. I think I might really like him, and after this week, I don't think I'm alone in my feelings."

Maybe longer, if I'm being honest. He's always flirted, skirted the edges of messing with me. And there was that one time he completely ignored Mrs. Mahoney's bombshell granddaughter. Each time I recall her confused look, as if no one had ever walked past her without a double take, a tiny thrill zings through me. Along with Las Posadas, it's in my top ten all-time favorite Danger Stevens moments.

Paige exhales, making the ticking noise with her tongue on the roof of her mouth she does when she's thinking. "Okay, so maybe you start with, 'Hey, I like you.' Ten bucks says he'll ask you out. Or with any luck, he'll kiss *your* face off. Win-win."

My stomach revolts at her ten-dollar ante. Whether in books or movies, bets are an icky trope.

"No wager. But fine—I'll try telling him," I say, frowning with a dash of whiny groaning as we say goodbye.

Yes, I'm being a baby about this.

But you try crushing on a boy who's the epitome of every fear your father instilled at the tenderest age of a girl's life, turn around and antagonize that boy for the next ten to twelve years, only to have him reappear after a six year absence a bearded hottie who's sweet and accommodating and doesn't blink an eye when you goad him into arguing with you about movies like the creepy film freak you are, and not catch feelings again.

Out of breath? Confused? Me too.

But also, not.

Because after doing the math after admitting exactly how long I've been fighting and denying my feelings for Danger Stevens, kissing his face off doesn't seem fast moving at all.

Sundays are our highest visiting days, so in my pre-holiday event-planning hubris, I thought a family-inclusive cookie decorating party would be a fun, festive activity. And it would have been, had I remembered to require reservations and have guests pre-pay the fee to offset our costs.

You know, and staff it properly.

Four times as many people as I was prepared for showed up this afternoon, so now I'm scrambling to assist our guests in the main dining room at Valle Encantado with a handful of staff I bribed with overtime. We need another ten people in the kitchen, but I'd settle for four.

Sadly, it's only me in here on what's supposed to be my day off, mixing dough and shoveling pans into the oven with haggard efficiency as the kitchen staff does their daily choreography for tonight's dinner service.

Do you know the feeling when you're alone in the dark and suddenly your arm and neck hair prickles at the sensation you're not actually alone? Usually, it turns out to be nothing more than a perfectly normal random house noise or maybe a pet, but you can't settle until you know for sure. That's how I feel as I measure ingredients for more cookie dough in the corner of the busy industrial kitchen. I glance over my shoulder, knowing who I want to see striding through the doors into the kitchen.

There's a smile on my face and a yearning in my chest to ditch the dough and tell Dan exactly how I feel, right here, right now. Only he's not alone, so I need to play it cool. Following him to the stainless-steel countertop I've claimed as my workspace are his mom, Grams, and Tory.

"You guys! What are you doing here?" I dust my dough-globby hands off on a kitchen towel before greeting each of the women with a hug.

"Dan said you might need some help," Grams says. "Where do you want us?"

My insides feel as if two flocks of birds take flight in opposing directions. One, a ballet of swans, light and happy with relief over not having to cut and bake three hundred more cookies myself. The other, a murder of crows, dark and suspicious. I'm unused to help, and I don't trust it. Especially when I'm managing quite capably on my own.

Except, weren't you just wishing for four more people?

True, but history and brain-wiring aren't always reliable, so forgive me for needing a second to right my thinking instead of leaning into old habits.

Dan hangs back from his family, most likely giving me space since whatever changed between us in Santa Fe is new and untested but different from before. It's weird how ready I am to test the waters now after keeping him at arm's length for so long.

My gaze locks onto his as I sidestep his family to greet him directly. His dark blond eyebrows climb upward with each step closer until I'm fully in his space. I've astonished him, which is amusing enough I'm already thinking how to shock him again. It's the same thrill I used to get with my petty digs, only without the niggle of remorse afterward.

Impulsively, I lift to my toes and wrap my arms around his neck. Paige's words this morning flit through my brain, but a kiss is not what I'm after. Though I'm growing more amenable to the idea as his hands graze my hips tentatively, like he's not sure how to handle this abrupt new addition to our relationship.

"You're quite the recruiter," I say with a grin, unable to tear my eyes from his. "How did you know I needed help but would never ask for it?"

"Have you ever asked for help before?" His knowing smirk has me rethinking which side of the kiss-or-claw fence I'm on.

"Hey, I called in extra staff today."

He chuckles. "How about people not in it for the overtime?"

"Nobody does anything without incentive."

"Oh? Explain them." He chin-nods toward his family.

I glance over my shoulder, fighting the urge to hide my face in his rather well-sculpted chest and feeling sheepish and silly for continuing to drape myself over Dan like this in front of them. From their matching smirks, they aren't the least surprised.

"Thank you," I say, including everyone, but especially Dan.

And then I kiss him soundly on the cheek before dropping my heels onto the floor.

I know. Totally not a "me" move, but I'm not exactly myself around him these days. I've never experienced this rush of feelings before and it's as exciting as it is disconcerting.

My arms turn to noodles as I release Dan and step back with impressive restraint to reach for the bowl of dough. Cool as a cucumber, that's me. Pay no attention to the trembling hands inverting said bowl onto the counter.

Where is the rolling pin? It was here a second ago.

Tory nudges the wooden cylinder out from against the side of the bowl... inches from my fingers.

"Thanks, Tory," I say, ultra composed and not at all red-faced.

She snickers.

Grams steps to the industrial sink and washes her hands after tying on an apron she retrieved from a canvas tote I failed to notice in my excitement to see Dan again.

"Put us to work, girlie. What are we making?"

The timer on the oven I'm using buzzes. Oof, we need to hurry before the cookies our pastry chef made on Friday run out. Why hadn't I anticipated more than fifty people attending when our community has close to four hundred?

"Tory, will you take the pans of biscochitos out of the oven and hurry them into the dining room? One pan to each of the two tables with bowls of cinnamon sugar. They'll need to dip the cookies while they're hot."

"On it!" she says, springing into action.

The traditional New Mexican spice cookies are for eating, not icing, but they'll keep everyone happy until I get more sugar cookies out to decorate.

The other three give me their full attention, causing me to stand a bit straighter. This commanding-the-troops feeling is amazing. Is having help always so gratifying? I could definitely get used to having help if this is how it works.

Surveying the tasks at hand and mentally assigning them to the best person for each, I ask, "Grams, will you oversee biscochitos?"

"Of course," she answers with a short nod. "Got a recipe card for quantities?"

"Right here." I slide the card across the counter to the waiting bowl and measuring cups. "Danny Boy, I'll roll this batch and you cut out shapes. Ms. Stevens, will you mix more sugar cookie dough?"

"Call me Lena," she says while slipping a second apron out of Grams's tote. Lena tosses me a wink before stepping up to the sink to wash her hands. "Or *Mom*."

Good grief. I'll admit I'm crushing on her son, but *Mom* is the definition of moving fast.

After my stomach quits flipping, the four of us settle into a rhythm easily, and I catch myself smiling at the sense of rightness. We get a groove going, and in no time at all, our corner of the kitchen is clean and Tory's delivering the last of the cookies.

Lena and Grams have already migrated into the dining room with Silas and Peggy. I peek through the small windows in the kitchen doors and smile at the roomful of happy families bopping their heads to Harry Connick Jr.'s Christmas swing playlist, swirling, sprinkling, and laughing together.

This is why I love my job. Why I love adding family-inclusive activities despite this being a 55+ active-life community focused primarily on adults living their best lives.

Events such as this remind me that everyone is welcome to the table in God's kingdom. On earth as it is in heaven, there's a seat for every heart who seeks Him—young, old, or in between.

But also, I remember how awkward it was to visit Nonno near the end. It killed me to watch him decline, and carrying on one-sided conversations was uncomfortable. Working on puzzles helped take away some of the pressure to talk. Even before then, hanging out with my grandparents was so much more fun when we had our hands busy. I loved to cook beside Nonna, to prune the roses and pull weeds with Nonno.

Tonight, there's no awkwardness. Everyone is having fun. Including crusty Mr. Greene, who I've only seen smile once in six years. Mrs. D'Angelo's three-year-old grandson offers him a mangled cookie, and instead of sneering, Mr. Greene beams at the child like it's the gift of a lifetime.

"You did well, Alley Cat," Dan murmurs at my back.

I lean into his warmth, and I'm delighted when he slides his arms around my waist in a gentle hug. The cacophony of kitchen sounds fades as I turn to face the man I'd ordinarily correct for using the nickname I've always hated.

Except it's growing on me.

In fact, I'm so content right now I might purr to give him a reason to keep using it.

"Thank you, Danger," I say softly, the fingers of my right hand tracing up his chest to fiddle with the button he's left undone near the top of his collared shirt.

His forehead dips to touch mine, and until this moment I've never appreciated why characters do this in romance scenes.

My heart's a cascade of winged creatures, and I'm not sure what we're doing anymore. This man is so much more than the box I tried to keep him in for all those years. He's kind and funny and handsome, and I love how he jumps right in to help the people he cares about.

Which I'm beginning to see includes me.

The realization emboldens me to lift my gaze to his.

Food prep continues in the background at a near frantic pace, and I know we'll need to get into the dining room any second to thank everyone for coming then get the place cleaned up before dinner service, but for now I can't break myself from this bubble of him and me in each other's arms. It feels so right.

Why did I waste so many years fighting this, fighting him?

He even smells good. Like sandalwood and cinnamon took a hike in a mountain of butter and sugar.

"Alley," he nudges my nose with his as the moment stretches and fills me with warmth until I want to curl up inside it forever.

"Yeah, Danny Boy?" I can't help it. Sorry not sorry.

He rewards me with a soft, cookie scented chuckle.

"I really like you."

Effervescent bubbles of happiness tempt me to shriek and dance in place, but the earnestness in Dan's eyes melts those bubbles into a warm gooiness.

He said it first, but I'm so ready to be brave and take my secret crush out of years of denial and into the open.

"I really like you too."

Chapter 16

Dan

The school vibrates with a hum of equal parts anticipation and fear with a splash of chaos—a contagious energy that began on Monday morning and has steadily grown more intense the closer we get to Wednesday's noon dismissal. I get it, though.

Three days have passed since I last saw Alessia, and I find myself growing as restless as the students, which is why I'm ditching out on the parent-sponsored faculty luncheon and heading straight to Valle Encantado as soon as the bell rings.

"Fifteen minutes." I call out the warning for my sake as much as the students'.

My two troublemakers in the back squirm in their seats, refocusing their attention on the essay question on the last page of their final exam. I walk one more observant lap around the room before returning to my desk and the book I've been reading.

As the dismissal bell sounds over the intercom, my tenth graders race to exchange their exam booklets for their phones from the lockbox on my desk and flee the room. I slide my book into my messenger bag, give the room a quick onceover before shutting off the lights, and lock the door.

Free at last.

After dodging and weaving through the throng of students, I'm halfway to the exit when our principal, Ms. Farouq, steps into my path. I feel like a kid getting caught ditching class with the way she holds her covered head high and stares down her nose at me, a feat for someone a head shorter than my five-feet-eleven.

"Leaving so soon, Mr. Stevens? Will you not attend the luncheon?" The censure in her tone gives me pause.

"I'm sorry, no. I have an appointment at one."

Which is true. I'm picking Alessia up to take her to the flower shop to find out if it's possible to import tropical flowers this time of year without spending the gross national income of a small country.

One precisely lined eyebrow lifts. "I see."

Uh oh, more censure. That does not bode well.

"This is not the first faculty social event you have missed, Mr. Stevens. Positive relationships within the faculty foster a supportive environment which is vital to the success of our school community. Have I made myself clear?"

"Yes, ma'am. I will make more of an effort to engage with my coworkers socially after the break."

"Excellent," she says with a regal air before dismissing me with a nod.

Air puffs from my cheeks as I finish my trek through the now empty hallway and out the doors to the parking lot. I had a feeling this might become an issue, but I'd been hoping to fly under the radar a little longer.

Alessia asked if there was another reason for leaving Texas when my family called about Brian's passing. There certainly was, and I have zero regrets about leaving. I also have no intention of forming relationships with anyone from work, either.

Been there, done that, and lost my job because of it.

"I'm in shock." Alessia sighs as we exit the flower shop. She elevates a flat, dramatically trembling hand. "Look at this. Actual shock!"

"Sticker shock," I roll my eyes, opening the passenger door. She's rubbing off on me. "Exaggerate much?"

As she climbs inside the SUV, Alessia screws up her face and sticks out her tongue. It's ridiculous, and much cuter than her eyerolls. I close the door and round the vehicle, returning the goofy face through the windshield. Her laughter washes over me as I climb into the driver's seat and blow onto my frozen fingers. I needed that sound after three days of exam energy and getting reprimanded earlier. It warms me faster than the old heater in this vehicle will.

"I can't go to Peggy and Silas with these numbers. They're on a fixed income!"

"Als, you do realize how much an apartment at Valle Encantado costs, right? That kind of lifestyle doesn't come cheap."

"I know, but—"

"All-inclusive active lifestyle community," I add, parroting their tagline. "It's not the kind of place people with limited income can afford to retire."

"Not true, Valle has options for—"

"I promise. Peggy's not going to feel the same sticker shock as you. She's loaded."

"Really?" She rears, eyes widening in surprise. "How do you know?"

"Silas was grousing about blowing money on a big theme wedding last week. Peggy threw a wet dishrag at his chest and said, 'what happened to *if that's what the love of my life wants, then that's what she'll have*, huh?'" I chuckle at the memory. "Then she told him it was her money, and she couldn't take it with her in the end, so why not. I've surmised from conversations with Silas that her family's money played a big part in why they broke up in the first place."

"I had no idea. She's not flashy about it."

"Most wealthy people aren't flashy. That's how they stay wealthy."

We head to Valle Encantado and greet Pam on our way to Ms. Peggy's apartment. Without warning, Alessia jumps with her hand raised above her head and slaps the top of the doorframe as we pass through. I didn't think anybody over the age of seventeen did that.

Her cheeks turn bright pink.

"What was that about?"

She shows me a small cluster of green pinched between her fingertips. "Mistletoe. I remove them, and somebody puts them back up. It's annoying!"

"Wait, you mean there's a Christmas decoration you *don't* want up?" The place is a veritable showcase of holiday décor thanks to her.

"It's *mistletoe*, Dan. What do you think?"

I trip over my own feet, barely managing to catch myself before plowing into Alessia, but she keeps walking—oblivious to the way her use of my name now has me following her like a panting stray.

She must notice I'm lagging behind. Cocking her head to the side, she gives me a raised eyebrow. "What?"

"First of all, this moment must be documented for posterity. Let the record show, at 5:08pm on Wednesday, December thirteenth, Alessia Catano first called me *Dan*."

I love her eyerolls. She follows it up with an adorably amused smile. "You're such a goof. What's the second?"

I grin. "What's wrong with mistletoe?"

Alessia groans dramatically. "So many things."

Each of which she enumerates the rest of the walk to Ms. Peggy's door. The older woman greets us with a warm smile and ushers us inside. Alessia glances around with her mouth falling into an awed O shape. I told her the woman had money.

The place is pristine, professionally decorated in varying shades of white, according to Grams. To me it just looks like white walls with white floral paintings, white furniture, and white knickknacks on white shelves. The stark white is broken up by the occasional glimmer of gold trim and dark orange throw pillows on either end of her sofa.

"Your home is beautiful, Ms. Peggy," Alessia says, still taking everything in. "I love all the windows."

"The windows are what sold me on this unit. Now, dear, what did the florist have to say?" Peggy ushers us to the loveseat and takes the adjacent chair. "Thank you both for going on my behalf. I've been slowing down, you know, and don't have the stamina for going out I used to."

A load of baloney. Ms. Peggy takes daily walks around the entire community. While she doesn't leave the property much anymore, she told me it's because she prefers her peaceful bubble over the pace of city life.

"We were happy to do it," Alessia says, patting the older woman's hand gently. "I mean, being surrounded by flowers in the middle of December? Such a hardship."

Peggy's laugh is as soft and sweet as the woman herself. The women talk through the floral details, which is great because Alessia took half a million pictures on her tablet, and I only retained about ten percent of what the florist said. Als shows the bride-to-be her final photograph—the official cost estimate including rush order fees and premiums for the holiday season and imported blooms.

"Did you get a second bid?"

Alessia nods. "This one is willing to give a ten percent discount since they deliver to the community regularly."

"They're a chain though, correct?"

"Yes, ma'am."

"Let's go with the local shop. I'd prefer to pay extra to support a small business."

"I wish more people did the same, Ms. Peggy. I'll be honest, their arrangements looked better too. A clear case of getting what you pay for."

"It usually is. Thank you for taking the time out of your busy schedule to handle this for me, sweetheart. My goodness! It's twenty after. I'm meeting Silas in the bistro at five-thirty. Would you two care to join us?"

"No, ma'am," I say, in case they've forgotten I'm still here. "We have plans."

Alessia's head whips around on her neck so fast she'll need a chiropractor. Before she outs me, I pump my eyebrows. She, of course, rolls her eyes.

"Well, wonderful!" Ms. Peggy gushes. "You two enjoy your date."

"Oh!" Alessia gasps. "It's not—"

"We will, thanks," I interject, leaning to give Ms. Peggy a quick hug goodbye before tugging Alessia out the door.

She's protesting before we're halfway down the hall.

"Dan, why did you let her think we're going on a date?"

I grab her by the hand and spin her to a stop with her back against the wall. Careful not to crowd her too much, I tilt her chin until our gazes meet.

"Alessia," I say darkly. She has no idea what she does to me. "That's the second time you've called me *Dan*."

Her eyes widen. "So?"

"So, I like you. You like me. I very much want to take you on a date. Tonight, or any other. What do you say?"

I watch her throat pulse around a swallow. She has a lovely neck, and one day soon I'm going to press my lips right on the tiny mole below her ear.

"Yes," she says on a feathery exhale, and it takes every ounce of restraint I can muster not to kiss her before we have a first date. Especially when she gives me a look like it's *me* she wants, not dinner.

"Great. Shall we?" I nod toward the exit.

At the next doorway, she groans, reaches up, and removes another green sprig, tossing it into the nearest receptacle.

"Oh, and Alley Cat?"

She tilts her head, waiting.

"You're wrong about the mistletoe."

Chapter 17

Alessia

This is the point I should probably explain my history with Danger Stevens. It's perfect timing since I'm hiding out in the bathroom while waiting for our table to be ready and all.

Why am I hiding in the bathroom?

Excellent question. I wish I had the answer.

Maybe because I AM ON A DATE WITH DANGER STEVENS.

I want to be here. I do. I'm only having a teeny tiny, itty-bitty freak out, that's all.

Because feelings.

They're bombarding me, making me feel all kinds of awkward right now. If I leave this bathroom before I've had sufficient time to get the *Everything Everywhere All at Once* level chaos that is my head fully sorted, this date's going to be weirder than the blind date Paige sent me on four years ago where the guy let one rip at the table and proceeded to make a case for normalizing flatulence.

I shudder to rid my mind of the foul memory.

Ahem, so, *history*.

I met Danger Stevens in sixth grade. The first year of middle school is a fresh kind of misery. You've just left the safety of elementary as the top dogs, and now it's a repeat of kindergarten, only with hormones. And those hormones hit everyone differently, and no one knows how to deal with them. Everything constantly feels SO BIG, the stakes higher than high.

Danger Stevens was the boy all the girls had a crush on. He had Jesse McCartney's eyes and Chad Michael Murray's hair and smile. Good student, fast runner. Comfortable in his own skin—or did a better job of faking it than the rest of us. Those days even *I* thought his name was cool. Best of all, he was *nice*.

So, when he started sitting next to me in social studies, talking to me as if I were the only girl in the world, it was only natural I developed a crush too. Unfortunately, shortly after I discovered boys could be fascinating and flirting could be fun, my world bottomed out.

Dad's multiple affairs and Paige's existence came to light, and suddenly I couldn't look at any male without wondering if he was destined to be the same kind of guy. My mom was a blindsided mess of tears and bitterness for the remainder of my formative years, which I'll admit left me more than a little jaded as well.

My crush on Danger persisted despite my extreme efforts to squash it. I watched from the sidelines as the same attention that had made me feel so special was lavished on other girls too, and it was more than my young heart could bear. So, I made a game of quips and digs to keep him in his place. To remind him not *all* the girls wanted to be kept on his leash.

Remember, though, Dan was nice. Especially to females.

He never actually strung anyone along. In truth, he didn't really date much in high school, and the few times I saw him with girls in college, he was the same respectable guy he always had been.

I know it now and I knew it then, but when a girl is drowning in huge, ugly, angry feelings for her father she can't express in a healthy fashion, she finds other ways to lash out. Namely at a boy who speaks charm and banter fluently and can do no wrong in the eyes of other women.

Like Daddy.

I'd like to take a moment to say a prayer of thanks for my therapist. She helped me unpack much of this years ago, and while I bounce my troubles mostly off my rabbit now, the skills I learned are the reason I'm melting down here in this bathroom instead of getting my kicks still tormenting Dan. Someday I pray for a nice, happy middle ground.

The bathroom door swings open as I finish washing my hands. The hostess, who tried (and failed, by the way) to flirt with Dan as she put us on the list, walks in.

"Your boyfriend is looking for you."

"Oh he's—" I cut off my own protest. It's none of her business what my relationship with Dan is.

Drying off my hands with a paper towel, I thank her and turn to leave, but my feet don't obey because I now realize I've been in here too long. He's going to think I have a gastrointestinal problem.

Oh my gosh, I already feel my face flaming.

I'm stuck in limbo. As much as I want to go out there and enjoy my first date with Danger Stevens—

That's it. I'm not giving up the full name. It's grown on me, and henceforth shall be used to refer to the crush version of the man.

Wait, so which version am I on a date with?

Both, genius.

I'm staying in here forever. He can't see me post-meltdown. He'll see my crazy and run the whole way back to Texas.

"Your table's ready. Has been, for like, five minutes." Hostess girl's sour attitude yanks me out of my meltdown, and now I'm embarrassed all over again.

"Sorry," I squeak and flee the restroom.

The hallway is mercifully long enough to compose myself and think of an excuse. It doesn't take long to spot Dan across the restaurant in a dimly lit corner. He smiles and stands when our eyes meet. I feel all glittery inside with an urge to pick up the pace.

Gosh, I really like him, don't I?

"Hey," he greets me warmly, pulling out my chair.

Because this is a *date*.

"I wasn't—" I stop myself before blurting about details best left unspoken on a date where food is present. "*You know.* In there."

Weirdly thumbing toward the restroom, I blather on. "I was washing my hands and giving myself a peptalk."

"Peptalk, huh?" He adds the smirky half-smile that used to tick me off (because I loved it, gah!).

"Needed more *intelligent conversation*?"

I love his recall of what I consider a Top 20 quip.

"Relax, Als." He rubs his hands up and down my arms from behind as I take my seat. "Doesn't take a mind reader to see you're nervous. Full confession, I am too."

He is? He looks so calm. Not fair.

"So how about this," he says, resuming his seat. "Let's simply enjoy our meal with conversation. No pressure. No expectations. Just two people who've known each other the better part of twenty years without ever truly knowing each other."

I don't understand why his words work, but my mind and body calm in a heartbeat.

"Okay." My response comes out on an exhale. "I can do that."

Our server brings an oblong white plate to the table. "Here are your eggrolls. On this end," she points a long, manicured nail to the closest corner. "We have two of our Burque rolls, which are stuffed with carne asada, green chile, and our house blend of carrots, jicama, taro, and bean threads. Next, we have our take on the fusion classic kimchi quesadilla in eggroll form. And on the far end are two traditional pork eggrolls filled with our house blend vegetables."

My eyes grow wider with each new description. I glance at Dan, and he's positively mesmerized.

"Thanks," he tells her without glancing up.

She smiles and saunters away. I notice the way Dan's eyes are fixed on me.

He gives me a sheepish grin. "Sorry for ordering without you. I wasn't sure how long you'd be and thought an appetizer would buy us some time to choose entrees."

"They look amazing." I reach for one of the traditional rolls first and sink my teeth into the crispy outer layer.

While I'm an adventurous eater, I've never been to a Latin-Asian fusion restaurant. The crunch is satisfying, but it's the blend of flavors inside that inspires a groan.

"Right?" Dan says with a grin, biting into one of the kimchi ones.

I try that one next, and while I'm not so sure about the texture, it's loaded with cheesy spicy goodness I devour greedily. By the time the server delivers our entrees—pad thai tacos for me, a sushiritto for Dan, and kamikaze fries to share—I'm in love.

"How did you find this place?"

He shrugs as though he hasn't completely changed my culinary future. "Couple of teachers at work."

Figures he'd have friends at work already. I mean, how can he not? The man's a people magnet.

"So, you've eaten here before? With your friends?"

"Oh, no. Coworkers. I overheard them talking about it. Sounded good, and I always dread the 'what do you want' merry-go-round."

"Me too. Glad you suggested this. I enjoy trying new places."

The food chips away the last of my awkwardness as we review our selections, playacting as food critics. He delivers a description of the kamikaze fries that's so spot on I wouldn't be shocked to learn he's one of those people who leaves detailed, novel-length reviews on Yelp. He is a word guy, after all. I am, however, taken aback at how hard he's got me cracking up.

Also, his presence inexplicably quiets my overactive mind. Have I ever noticed before?

I'm noticing other things, too.

The way he gives me his full attention, for one. The fact he hasn't noticed our hostess playing refill-bringer instead of our server or how she leans so far forward I fear she'll have a wardrobe malfunction isn't lost on me.

My favorite, though, is how easily the conversation flows once I'm not stuck inside my head or trying too hard. He's always brought out my snarky side, but now I have this desire to tell him all kinds of crazy things I wouldn't normally share with anyone but Paige.

I tried dating for a while. Never clicked with anyone enough to push myself past the awkwardness or desire to stay home on the couch in my jammies with Audrey HepBun. Tonight's been a welcome change.

It's late by the time he takes me to my car in the Valle Encantado parking lot. In the pitch dark, he insists on rounding the vehicle to get my door and "see me safely inside."

Who does that anymore?

I'm fumbling to find my keys at the bottom of my purse, which of course brings to mind the porch scene in *Hitch*. I glance at Dan, wondering if he's considering going ninety percent. Do I want him to?

It's hard to see in the poorly lit parking lot, which I absolutely need to bring up to the maintenance crew at the next staff meeting, but I think he could be leaning. You know, like *While You Were Sleeping* leaning. What do I do?

It's been how many years since I've been kissed?

I'm frozen in freakout mode again, but Dan somehow understands and makes everything better by wrapping his wonderful arms around my body and tugging me close.

"I like you, Alessia," he murmurs near my ear. I shiver, and he gently tightens his hold though it wasn't from the cold. "No pressure, no expectations, remember? Getting to know you better tonight was enough."

His words or his voice, I don't know which—maybe both—give me the freedom to breathe. To simply exist in this moment.

To be brave.

"I like you too, Dan," I say softly now that my body is obeying me again. My hands find their way up, through his open coat, to his chest the way they did the other night in the kitchen. My mind is calm and clear as twilight after the rain, and I know exactly what I want.

"No pressure. No expectations. But..." I inhale a fortifying breath. "I'm gonna need you to kiss me now."

Chapter 18

Dan

She doesn't have to ask twice, but after wanting this kiss for so long, I am absolutely going to take my time.

Alessia's hands are warm on my chest as she lets her fingers trace the smooth edges of my shirt's open top button. I doubt she knows what she's doing to me. It reads like an unconscious action, but she's driving me crazy in the best way.

The faint glow from the lights gives her an angelic aura, the kind of glow and beauty that inspired eighteenth century men to write sonnets. She's easily the most alluring woman I've ever known.

I bring one hand up to the middle of her back and the other to the juncture of her head and neck. I've always wondered if her hair was as soft as it looked. Now I know, and I pray God in His mercy keeps my sweaty hand from sticking to it.

Long black lashes drift closed as her chin tilts upward ever so slightly. Her warm breath skims my face with a hint of the Andes mints our server left with the check. It's a cold December night, but it feels like spring with her in my arms.

Closing the distance, I skim the side of her face with mine.

She giggles under her breath. "That tickles."

"Sorry," I murmur, doing it again with less pressure. "Better?"

"Heavens, yes," pours out her lips in a rush.

My lips curve up into the beginning of a smile, and I'm not sure how much longer I can hold out. I will, though, because moments such as these are meant to be savored. Some guys press too fast for the "good stuff." Maybe it's how I was raised, or my love of literature, but this right here *is* the good stuff.

"You're stunning, Als."

"Dan?"

"Mm-hmm?" I could stand here nuzzling her the rest of the night. Every nerve ending is electrified, every heartbeat a rush.

"Please shut up and kiss me already."

This woman.

I think I love her.

Smiling and feeling like I could conquer the world if she asked, I find her lips and lose all thought.

My entire being is focused on this moment. Eyes closed, my other senses tune into the faintest details as her silky soft lips meet mine. The citrusy smell of her hair, the press of her fingers wrapped around my collar. The tiny hums of pleasure she gives, the taste of chocolate and mint on her tongue.

No kiss compares to this. To the surge of emotion roaring up from deep within, ferocious and fierce. Steady and true. She's who I want to kiss for the rest of my life.

Alessia's hand curls around my neck, and I swallow a groan as her fingers toy with the hair at my nape. As much as I want this to continue, it's time to throttle back and say goodnight. We have plenty of time to explore ahead of us.

She lets out a frustrated whimper when I break the kiss. I give in and press my lips to hers once more, lightly this time so we don't get lost again.

I'm not ready to let her go. It's inevitable, but I want to keep her here in the circle of my arms until the last possible second.

Foreheads touching, breaths mingling, I kiss the tip of her cold nose. "Thank you for not pushing me away."

Her smile lights up the night, but she says nothing.

"Please text me when you get home, so I know you're safe."

Alessia nods before unlocking and opening her driver's side door. She lingers a moment, a clear sign she wants one last kiss as much as I do. I'm no fool. Well, maybe her fool.

"G'night, Alley Cat."

She smiles as she takes her seat behind the wheel, her eyes peering up at me with affection. The look seizes my chest.

"Goodnight, Danger."

Groaning, I close her door and wave as she drives away.

I've never liked my name so much as when she says it.

"Are you sure about this?" I nod toward the doors leading into the community fitness center.

"Not really, but we don't exactly have a choice."

Alessia closes her eyes and inhales for a three count before exhaling on four. I reach for her hand, lacing our fingers together. The touching aspect of our relationship is still so new and exhilarating, I find myself wondering if I fell off a bridge into the Rio Grande and this is some Jimmy Stewart-esque parallel existence. Clarence has yet to make an appearance, so there's a chance Alley Cat's mine for real.

"Come on, Als. We've got this."

She squints one eye open, scrunching her nose up in a bunny face. I smile, having been introduced to her rabbit this morning when we dropped off the wedding favor supplies we'd purchased earlier in the day. They say pets resemble their owners—both are adorable.

"You'd better not step on my toes." Even her fake frowny face is cute.

I am so gone.

"Don't worry. I know what I'm doing. The question is, do you?"

Alessia scoffs. "Please. If you're so skilled, Mr. Astaire, let's see what you've got." She motions toward the door. "After you."

"No, no," I insist. "You first, Ginger."

I follow her into the fitness room, which this afternoon will serve as our dance space. Silas claims his dance skills are rusty, so he asked if we'd be willing to help him polish up before the wedding to surprise Peggy.

Naturally, Alessia is all-in because "who can resist such a romantic gesture," and I'm here because there's a one hundred percent chance of twirling my girl across the dance floor and showing her my moves.

Yes, I've got moves. You don't walk away from living with five ambitious, romance-loving women (seven if you count Aunt Mindy and Candice's periodic stays) without learning some form of dance. I'm just grateful Tory went through a swing dancing phase and not ballet.

Silas went all out and hired a pair of instructors, and to ensure there's no chance of discovery, enlisted Peggy's daughter to take her to lunch.

The man's got game, I'll give him that.

Silas and Peggy are from the Watusi, twist, and mashed potato era, but since it's their wedding, Cody, the male instructor, suggests a partner dance is more appropriate. He introduces his partner, Kendall, and the pair demonstrate a few options to test Silas's mobility and interest.

At the first mention of ballroom style, Silas grunts.

"Don't care to dance like I got a stick up my—" at Alley's bugged eyes, Silas corrects to "spine."

The man shakes his head at the waltz and downright refuses to tango but seems open to learning a little west-coast swing. The latter is an excellent choice for an elderly couple, since the movement is focused within a back-and-forth slot requiring minimal movement at a slower pace than east-coast.

"If you're ready, we'll begin with a simple box step." Cody says from the front of the room near the wall-mounted sound system while Kendall takes up her starting position with Silas.

Having Alessia in my arms compensates for the two and a half hours spent traipsing through Hobby Lobby. Shoulders squared, hand in hand, we flow through the basic motions until Cody chuckles and moves us on to the next set of steps. He corrects our form a few times, but otherwise seems content to let us goof around on our own while he focuses on helping Kendall with Silas.

Before long, I'm twirling Alessia around the perimeter of the room in a slowed down version of the Lindy Hop. She picks up the steps quickly, and after the first spin has her laughing with delight, I'm adding others, as well as a few of the simpler tricks I learned in class with Tory.

I forgot how much fun swing dancing is, but as it's coming back to me, I'm thinking how fun it'll be to take her out and show her some of the more advanced moves.

Glancing over to check on Silas, he's clearly uncomfortable with Kendall. She's young and pretty, but I'm guessing her energy is more than the man was prepared for. She keeps teasing him as if that'll put him at ease. Spoiler alert, it won't.

"He looks miserable," Alessia says breathlessly as I twirl her out and in, flush against me but watching our friend.

"Yeah," I agree. I keep sneaking peeks to check on him, but she's right.

Silas looks more distressed as the minutes pass. Kendall keeps grasping his hand and pinning it to her waist when Silas tries to hold both her hands instead.

An idea sparks. It's so obvious, I wonder why I didn't think of it from the start. "Hey, Cody?"

The guy crosses to us in three strides. "What's up? You guys look great out there. Have you been dancing together long?"

"No, first time," I say, shaking my head clear. I had a purpose here. "Silas loves westerns and country music. I bet he'd do better with a two-step, then add some country swing when he gets the hang of it."

Cody's face brightens into a broad smile. "Great idea, man. Kendall! Let's try something else."

He explains the plan, and I breathe easier when Silas's shoulders relax. This is good. I wish I'd have thought of it sooner.

"You're pretty smart, there, Danny Boy." Alessia flashes my favorite sassy smirk.

"Why, thankee, ma'am," I drawl, tipping an imaginary hat. "Shall we?" At her nod, I lead us in a slow two-step to match the tempo of the song Cody changed to for Silas.

She's grinning and laughing so brightly, she's making me dizzy, and I'm not the one spinning around the floor. I love the way her ponytail swings out behind her like a whip each time I twirl her body.

This moment right here makes every dance lesson I ever complained about totally and completely worth it.

Don't tell Tory I said so.

"Is there anything you don't do well?" she laughs.

"Resist you?" I say with a shrug and a half smile.

"Well now, that's not fair. You're turning a strength into a weakness to make yourself look good." Her brown eyes glimmer with humor, and I'm thinking about excusing ourselves out into the hall and claiming those lips again.

It's been two days, which is two days too long in my book.

Her gaze turns heated, and I'm about to tug her through the door when Cody calls out.

"Time to try something else. Silas still isn't comfortable. No offense, Kendall, but I think we'll need to switch partners. Silas might relax if he knows the person he's dancing with."

I glance at Alessia, but she's staring Kendall down. When my gaze shifts to the other woman, I see why. Kendall's wearing an all-too-pleased smile that makes me feel like a squirrel under the watchful gaze of the neighborhood hawk.

Alessia's expression softens as she catches the relief on Silas's face. "C'mon, Silas. Spin me around. Pretend I'm Peggy, and we'll be fine."

Guess that leaves me with Kendall. I wonder if I could fake an injury two bars into the song.

"I've seen your moves. Let's go, cowboy." Kendall grabs my hands and leaves me no choice once Cody turns on a country song I've never heard. Sounds like a recent one-hit wonder, but then these days they all do. I miss the stuff Silas used to play when I was a kid.

Does that mean I'm getting old? I haven't yet hit thirty.

Whatever. Music and movies aren't as good anymore, a fact that has nothing to do with my age. Means I have taste.

"Hey, Cody," I call. This time he stays at the stereo. "Play us some Travis Tritt, would ya?"

Cody's brow scrunches when the name doesn't register, but he taps his phone screen a few times until a familiar old song with a decent beat begins.

I find the rhythm and give Kendall a spin, but then she takes the lead and starts forcing me into more complicated moves. Sure, I know how to do them, I just don't want to do them with anyone but Alessia. Our relationship is too new, and I've worked too hard this month to prove I'm not the guy she thought.

No way am I risking hurting her feelings.

From the corner of my eye, I spy Silas ushering Alley into a basic turn. He catches the downbeat and resumes the steps like an old pro. In a few bars, he's even doing a few old school country swing combos that restore Alessia's smile.

She's gorgeous from the inside out. Silas's problem wasn't the steps, it was the woman. And while my body may be dancing with the wrong one, my attention is one hundred percent on the girl who's always been right for me.

Chapter 19

Alessia

Bliss.

That's the emotion I'm trying to focus on despite my weirdo brain waking me up with intrusive thoughts in the wee hours. Sharing my days with Dan this week has been sheer bliss.

After Saturday's dance lesson, Dan invited me to his church on Sunday morning. I had no idea he sang with the band. His church is a bit more contemporary than mine, but I enjoyed it, and the message was both sound and uplifting. Afterward, we decorated his house for Christmas, since I finished mine two weeks ago.

Monday, we had one more dance lesson with Silas, who's remembered his old moves. Thankfully, the athletic dancing goddess, Kendall, wasn't available. When I said as much, Dan replied, "Kendall who?" and swept me around the room until I forgot anyone existed but us.

While the rest of the week has been filled with wedding errands and to-dos—assembling favors since Peggy's arthritis has been flaring up with the cold, for starters—we've also had relaxing moments over shared meals as we get to know each other better. Then there's the kissing.

Cue swoony sigh with all the heart eyes.

Honestly, if my brain could wake me up replaying the highlight reels of our kisses, I'd never complain about lost sleep.

If only I were so lucky.

Instead, my dreams run wild with stuff like trapping myself in the storage room and missing Christmas with Paige because I'm buried under a life-sized Easter Bunny.

Then there was the one where my dad had his bandmates kidnap his assorted progeny, forcing us into a "fun, old-fashioned family Christmas." That one might've been the result of streaming a truly awful made-for-TV suspense followed by *Christmas Vacation*.

Last night's dream, though... Hours later, it still feels real, and I'm having trouble telling myself it's only in my head.

To understand why the dream freaked me out, I should rewind to the hours before I slept.

The evening started out pleasantly with a Christmas tree-lit romantic dinner at my place followed by *Rise of the Guardians* (a truly underappreciated animated film, if you ask me). Afterward, Dan and I snuggled on the couch as our conversation drifted to our dating histories. There wasn't much to either of ours, but something in the way he talked about the last woman he dated made me uneasy. Especially since I didn't get to ask enough questions before a text came in from Tory, asking us to meet the family at the hospital to pray.

Mave had a headache, heartburn, and majorly swollen hands and feet—commonplace on their own, but together can be symptoms of preeclampsia, which she's at higher risk for, thanks to her gestational diabetes. She and the baby are perfectly fine, praise God. Nothing more than dehydration and fatigue from putting in too many hours on her feet at work.

I didn't crawl into my bed and crash until after two in the morning. My dreams put us right back in the hospital, but the patient changed from Mave to Paige to Peggy, then Silas, and eventually Dan, each one dying of something different. Black shadows filled the edges of each horrifying part of the dream, curling in wisps of mist until Pitch (the boogeyman-inspired villain from *Guardians*) appeared, mocking me in Jude Law's terrifyingly pristine accent.

There's a scene in the movie where Pitch basically taunts Jack Frost about the answers to his questions remaining out of reach, how he'll never be accepted by the other guardians and always be a disappointment. It's chilling, the way he preys on Jack's fears.

I don't remember the exact words he said to me, but now that I'm awake hours later with a cup of tea on my porch safely inside a burrow of blankets, I recall him directing a similar monologue to me. Because of my faith, I also know my enemy isn't an animated being or a real-life person. In those predawn hours after first waking, I managed to pray myself back to sleep, yet the shadows still lurk in the corners of my mind even now.

The shadows have a name: fear. I know this. But knowing your enemy is only one step on the road to defeating them.

Truth is an ally, and so is love. But since one of the hardest parts of love is the fear of losing it... see my struggle here? Hard to hold on to bliss and the sweet honeymoon phase bubbles of joy and rainbows when fear sparks anxieties I've been fighting my whole life.

Am I enough? I must not be, why else would both my parents eschew time with me for their new families?

Am I too much? I've been told that often enough.

Why does Dan want to be with me?

Will everything work out okay for Mave and the baby, for Silas and Peggy's wedding, for my family, for the other residents who are so dear to my heart?

Heavy questions for nine in the morning.

I should've been up and moving hours ago, but it was such a late night, I knew I'd get nothing accomplished today without some rest. As soon as I finish my morning chai, I'll go inside and do something about this wad of tangles too greasy to pass for a cute messy bun anymore.

Audrey thumps the bottom of her hutch in warning. Tilting my head to the side, I listen for whatever disturbed her. Sounds like someone setting up a ladder. Bet it's one of my neighbors putting their Christmas lights up late. Honestly, it's December twenty-first—why bother?

My feet carry me around to the side of my house where I peek over the gate for a better look. Somebody's really going for it, and it's got to be close. Scraping, dragging, thudding, then the slam of a tailgate moments before feet clamber up the ladder. The noise echoes on the crisp morning air, making it hard to tell exactly where it's coming from, but I'd say somewhere close.

Oof. I glance at my phone, and the time tells me I'd better hurry up if I want to get today's activity set up on time. We're doing Holiday Game Night with several different activities, so I'll need two hours minimum.

After a rushed shower that left my skin pink and toasty, I throw on a silly pair of printed leggings Paige sent me as a joke three years ago. They're brown camouflage, but the camo pattern is made up entirely of reindeer. Pairing it with an oversized white crewneck sweatshirt with a red-nosed Rudolph face and some fuzzy socks, I feel ridiculous but also cute, in an over-the-top festive way.

Normally I wouldn't be caught dead dressed in this, but a few of our more outlandish residents suggested we add a "spirit week" to the calendar similar to their grandkids' schools. It's been fun to see so many residents get into it with White Out, Christmas Tree Day, and Ugly Sweater Day. In case it's not obvious, today is Reindeer Day.

I'm debating whether to add a headband with antlers I found at the dollar store when the clang of a ladder sounds right outside my bedroom window. Barely stifling a shriek, I peek through the miniblind slats.

What on earth is that man doing?

In less than a minute, I'm out the door and staring up the ladder at one thermal wearing Danger Stevens. The man rocks a pair of sweats, let me tell you.

"Why are you putting colored lights on my eaves?"

Dan practically jumps out of his skin, barely managing to catch himself before plunging off the ladder to his death. Okay, not death, but certain injury since the only cushion for his potential fall is a bunch of dead mums I neglected to clear out.

"Alessia!" He gasps. "You're supposed to be at work already."

"Slept in, which is what I thought you'd be doing."

"Oh. Yeah, I tried, but Tory's car wouldn't start, and she needed a ride."

I give him a raised eyebrow. "That still doesn't explain what you're doing here. At my house. On a ladder." Folding my arms across my chest (it is so much colder out here than it looks), I huff a sigh. "Will you please climb down and explain? Talking up to you is killing my neck."

"So, you're saying I'm a pain in the neck?" Dan grins as he descends the ladder.

I roll my eyes and smile when he skips the last two rungs and lands with a thud in front of me. "You said it, not me."

His smile crinkles the corners of his eyes. It's a great smile and my heart skips a beat. "Morning." He bends and presses a light kiss to my lips.

Much as I'd prefer to explore his mouth further, I really do need to get moving. But first, I need answers. This man is far too good at weaseling out of answering my questions.

"So?"

His brow furrows. "So... what?"

"Why are you putting lights on my house mere days before Christmas?"

He shrugs, and I consider whether to pinch him or flick him in the forehead if he avoids any longer. Dan lets out a longsuffering sigh before gracing me with an annoyed look.

"The other night, you said one of the parts you missed most about the holidays since your parents split was the feeling of living inside a gingerbread house. Thought I could surprise you with a bit of nostalgia after work tonight."

Somebody call Oliver because I'm a bowl of mush, and the poor child wants some more.

How do I respond to a gesture so sweet? No one has ever done something like this for me.

Oh my word, am I tearing up?

"Oh, honey, don't cry." Dan sweeps me into his arms, squeezing me tight against his chest. "I'll put it all away if it upsets you."

Can he get any sweeter?

"No!" Regaining some semblance of control, I try again in a normal tone. "No, please. I love it."

"Yeah?"

I nod. "So much. You're the best boyfriend ever."

He grips my arms and thrusts me backward, halting my impending freak out over saying the wrong thing by grinning the widest smile I've ever seen. Big enough to see molars. He laughs before pulling me flush against him into a hug so tight I may pop.

"What is happening right now?" I murmur, totally confused.

"You called me *boyfriend*."

Was I not supposed to? I mean, he doesn't look upset, but I could be reading him wrong. My fingers start tingling, and not because Dan's holding them. "I know we haven't talked about it, but—"

"Oh, no. By all means. I love the title."

Spiral averted. I can breathe.

"Me too," I admit, the relief and joy causing my lips to twitch with the beginning of a smile.

It's so weird how less than a month ago, I thought I loathed this man. Now, I wonder if I'm on my way to loving him. He's so much more than I used to believe, but am I?

"So," he's still grinning, "permission to kiss my girlfriend?"

He's such a goof. I can't remember the last time a person made me smile so easily. Or felt my heart thump so erratically.

"By all means," I say, echoing his earlier phrasing.

Dan wastes no time claiming my mouth like a hungry man at a steak buffet. Except less messy and more intentional because that initial image was kind of gross. And what he's doing with his tongue is anything but gross. It's exquisite, and I'm falling down a rabbit hole of sensations that are deliciously vibrant and fizzy and *bliss*.

Why'd I have to think of that word again? Now I'm battling the shadows, remembering my dream, the darkness, and the fear—

"Als?" He murmurs against my mouth.

"Mm-hmm?" I can't think straight when his beard hairs tickle the bottom of my lips.

"Tell your brain to be quiet a minute and focus on the task at hand, huh?"

With one hand gently pressing me to him and the other buried in my hair, Dan's touch brings the present into sharp focus. This moment with my newly minted boyfriend who's willingly facing the frigid December weather to transform my house into a gingerbread wonderland is the only thing worthy of my attention.

I concentrate on the softness of his lips and the delightful roughness of his beard, and the shadows finally dissipate.

Chapter 20

Dan

Laughter is the first sound to reach my ears as I stride through the halls of the main building at Valle Encantado in search of Alessia. It's a chorus of guffaws, chortles, and giggles that dares the Grinch himself to resist joining.

One laugh in particular rises above the rest. Peering through the inset windows in the doors to the common area, my vision zeroes in on Alessia at the head of a semi-circle of chairs, wearing her antlers and sporting a bright red clown nose—an addition she wasn't wearing earlier when she left me outside her house clipping strands of lights to the eaves. It's adorable.

She's adorable.

Her dark hair sways in a curtain as she throws her head back in a hearty laugh with Silas and another older guy I've never met. Folding a slip of paper and tucking it into her pocket, she closes her eyes and raises seven fingers. She shuffles hunched over a mimed cane, then spins and points to her antlers before running in place. The women on the other side of the room begin shouting as Alessia returns to her old woman with a cane stance, grimaces in horror, and falls to the floor in a classic playing dead pose.

Seeing an opportunity to slip inside unnoticed, I amble silently toward the semicircle. A timer beeps, and Alessia jumps up. The women groan as the men cheer.

"Seriously?" She playfully puts her hands on her hips. "It was 'Grandma Got Run Over by a Reindeer'!"

The handful of men to my left—her right—chuckle. One calls, "Point for us."

Alessia jogs to a nearby whiteboard and adds a point to their tally, but the women are still ahead by two.

"Danny Boy!" Silas booms.

Alessia jolts and flashes me a warm smile. I'll never tire of her smiles. Nope, not ever.

"Hey," she says shyly.

"Hey," I reply, edging closer to press a kiss to her temple. "How's my *girlfriend*?"

May sound juvenile, but that won't stop me from using the honorific any chance I get. She rolls her eyes playfully as the crowd behind us launches into catcalls.

"Saw that!"

"Aren't they cute?"

"Young love is precious."

"When's the wedding?"

Alessia's eyes widen at that one. No doubt my face is on fire. I glance over at Silas, who gives me a knowing smirk.

"Come on, kid." Silas pats an empty chair beside him. "You're on the men's team."

"What are we playing?"

I survey the common area, and in each of the four corners of the large room there are games going on. From the looks of it, this one is the most popular.

"Christmas carol charades," one of the women answers. "You're up since the others have had a turn."

With a nod, I reach into the bowl proffered by one of the men I've seen around but whose name slips my memory and retrieve a slip of paper. Unfurling it, my brow scrunches.

"Here goes nothing."

I hold up five fingers, and Silas calls, "five words!"

With a nod, I form a giant O with my arms and drop to my knees. How do I emulate a town? I zigzag with my hands low to the ground hoping it resembles tiny houses, because other than this, I've got nothing. Cradling my arms to mime holding an infant, I flash the men a desperate look.

"'O Holy Night!'" Mr. Greene shouts.

"That's only three words, Stanley," another grumbles.

"O Christmas… Baby?" He tries again.

"Not even a real title." Not sure where the retort came from.

I repeat the hand motions, making my roofline still smaller.

"Time!" Alessia calls.

Man, I wanted to win a point for the guys. "'O Little Town of Bethlehem,'" I say, shoulders sagging.

Alessia marks a point for the women. One of them whoops.

They're a wild bunch today.

The doors open, and Ms. Peggy beelines for our group as quickly as her feeble legs can carry her. Silas scoops her into his arms and dips her backward into a kiss. The grin he's sporting as they straighten is sheer pride.

"Still got it," he crows. I didn't miss the subtle twist he gave to stretch his lower back, though.

"Oh, you," Ms. Peggy chides, waving him off as they part ways and wearing a pleased smile.

Mr. Greene elbows me in the ribs. "Now that's how you kiss your woman hello."

"I'll keep that in mind." Truth.

Peggy joins the women's team with a breathless flush. I glance at Alessia. She's fixed on Peggy with an expression that matches my thoughts exactly.

I want a love like theirs when we're eighty.

Alessia swallows and averts her gaze, and I wonder about the cloud I saw behind her smile right before she turned away.

She can't still be doubting me—us—can she?

I conduct an inconspicuous study of her the rest of the afternoon and into the evening as we join Silas and Peggy for dinner to discuss the final details of their wedding. Alessia excuses herself early, something about palm trees.

"Go help her." Ms. Peggy nudges like she's read my mind.

"On it." I already intended to follow after Alessia, but I'm glad our friends aren't offended by our hasty exit.

Something is bothering Alley, and I want to know what. Correction, I *need* to know. Our relationship has been building in the right direction since Santa Fe, and after adding labels and sealing it with a rather memorable kiss, I thought we were on the right track. Clearly, I've missed something.

I'm growing desperate, but I can't find her anywhere. She's not in her office, not in the other two on-site restaurants. Not in the pool house where the wedding will be. I check the library, the common area, and circle around to the dining room and peer into the kitchen.

Nowhere.

I heave a relieved sigh when I hear her muttering to herself inside the storage room. The door is partially propped open by one of those wooden wedges Tory has for her classroom, only Alessia's is something off one of Tor's Pinterest boards. I almost laugh because the intricately painted design is so very *Alessia*. No plain Jane hunk of wood for my girl.

I rap my knuckles on the doorframe, but she doesn't notice.

Clearing my throat, I switch tactics to lighten the mood. "Enjoying more intelligent conversation, are we?"

A soft thud is followed by a string of Italian-sounding words I'm guessing aren't exactly PG. Those are always the first anyone learns with a second language. She sighs.

My body craves the reassurance of having her in my arms. I can't wait another second to hold her, so I fling open the door and trip over something, barely catching myself before falling headlong into a tall metal shelving unit loaded with plastic bins.

The door slams closed as I turn to reach for Alessia, but she doesn't collapse against my chest as I expect. She's staring at the door like it's a ship sailing past the island she's marooned on, hope extinguishing as the vessel grows smaller in the distance.

Ouch. That look is a little extreme, even for her.

Guess I'll dive right in. Can't fix what I don't know is broken. "Alley? What's wrong?"

She crosses her arms and lets out another sigh heavier than the first. "You locked us in, ding-dong."

Confused, I glance toward the door and back. "It doesn't open from the inside?" Then, because I'm a genius, I march to the door and jiggle the handle.

She snorts. "Such a man."

Rude.

"Yeah, and?" I retort, then catch myself. "Sorry."

This isn't an ideal situation, but we need to figure it out together without biting each other's heads off.

"I'm sorry too," she says, sliding to sit on the concrete floor. She nods toward the doorknob. "It needs a key to open from either side. That's why I prop it open."

Whoever installed this brilliantly thought out plan needs their head examined.

"Okay, so where are your keys? You had to use them to get inside, right?"

She exhales through loose lips making a lip-trill like the vocal warmups we used to do in choir—only instead of notes, hers resembles a horse greeting. It'd be cute if she didn't look so forlorn.

"Pam couldn't find hers, so I loaned her mine."

"So, she knows you're in here. Call her." I take a seat beside Alessia and bump her shoulder with mine. "Brr. Floor's cold."

She reaches into the shelf behind her and pulls out a folded canvas tarp. We each take an end and create a makeshift pallet, then she hands me her phone. I chuckle when the screen remains black.

"Of course. I mean, why wouldn't your battery die while we're stuck inside a locked supply closet? Isn't this a trope or something?"

Alessia snickers. "Trope, cheap plot device. Whatever you call it, it's stupid. Right up there with the whole 'only one bed'."

"Tory's favorite," I chuckle as I slide my arm behind her and tug until she drops her head against my shoulder. "Want to tell me why you fled to the storage room?"

"I didn't flee."

I kiss her temple. "Okay."

If she wants to pretend, I'll play along.

Or not. After two solid minutes of silence, I'm over it.

"Now may I ask what was bothering you tonight?"

"Ugh, you're not going to let me off the hook, are you?"

"Not really, kitty. Caring about you comes with that boyfriend title you bestowed earlier."

I can't see her face, but the shift of her cheek against my shirt feels like a smile. I'm about to give her another nudge when she employs a tactic I'm well-versed in myself: changing the subject.

"Pam's not coming." Alessia shifts within the crook of my arm, draping her forearm across my middle.

Her fingers toy with the lowest button on my open flannel. Always has to keep moving, this one.

"She texted me before my phone died to say she was so sorry, but she went home and forgot she left my keys at her desk. I didn't think it was important with the doorstop safely in place, but then, I didn't plan on a clodhopper barreling inside."

"Clodhopper?" I laugh, mildly offended. "Never heard anyone but my grandma use that word. Maybe Silas."

"Another seniorism I must've picked up here." Her chuckle comes out throaty. "What about your phone?"

Having already checked my pockets, I grimace before admitting, "I left it at the table."

"What? How?"

"You fled, remember?" I kiss the top of her head and give her body a gentle squeeze. "I needed to know you were okay."

"We're a couple of messes."

"Truth. So, since we're stuck here till someone mounts a rescue..." I let the nudge linger.

Alessia harrumphs, the vocal equivalent of her pouty frown.

"Fine," she fake grouses. "My head? It's a disaster zone. We're talking, all four lanes of the interstate zigzagged with orange barrels and no speed limit signs. Sometimes I get trapped inside an intrusive thought and it's difficult to refocus my attention on the right things or tasks."

"That bothers you?"

"Shouldn't it? I mean, it doesn't seem normal to work myself into a frenzy of self-doubt and worst-case scenarios."

"Part of what makes you, *you*. Who decides what's normal anyway?"

"Um, normal people?" Her eyerolls speak volumes. This one embodies the full force of her added "Duh."

It's not easy to suppress my smile, but I'm keenly aware of the potential consequences should I fail. "Okay, Miss Stubborn, then what is this 'normal' you believe you're supposed to be?"

"I don't know, but it's not whatever mess I've got happening up here." Alessia scrunches her fingers at the side of her head.

Bending the knee closest to her, I shift to make room for her to sit between my legs. She moves without argument, thankfully, and I breathe easier as she relaxes into the circle of my arms. I kiss the outer edge of her cheekbone.

"God made your brain to work exactly the way it does. With a purpose and a plan. He doesn't make mistakes."

"I know, but—"

"No *but*s. You're perfectly wonderful as you are."

Alessia reclines more fully against my chest. My butt's going to go numb here any minute, but I don't complain, and I won't be moving anytime soon. Getting her to talk like this is worth any discomfort I may endure.

I don't expect one simple conversation to fix everything that's been inside her head for so long, but I do hope I've added to the existing groundwork of Truth making it easier to accept she's lovable as is, for who she is.

We sit this way until my toes start to tingle. I tap her on the arm. "Hey, I need to stand."

"Yeah," she says as though it's painful to admit. "Me too."

She accepts my proffered hand once I rise to my dead feet. I intentionally tug too hard at the last minute, so momentum thrusts her against my waiting body. Her delighted laugh is contagious.

"Hmm. Right where I wanted you," I murmur into her ear.

I'm seconds from kissing her when she jabs her fingers into the sensitive skin above my hip. Despite my notable manliness, I shriek. In my defense, though, hips are prime tickle territory.

"You really want to go there, Alley Cat?"

"Meow," she purrs, jabbing her claws in again, wiggling until I squirm.

My arms pin her to me, but she's fast on her feet (as cats usually are), and soon we're an upright tangle of motion until she trips over the stray doorstop and careens us into a shelving unit on the other side of the small space. A bucket on the top shelf wobbles onto its side, spilling its contents in a rain shower of—

"Is that mistletoe?" I reach for the cluster of green plastic with white berries stuck to her shoulder.

My gaze scans the floor, mentally calculating bunches. There is at least a dozen, and a quick peek into the toppled bucket reveals three more.

"Somebody paid for those bunches," she shrugs. "I threw away the first few, but after a while I wondered if I should find the culprit and return them."

I love her mind.

Also, I probably ought to tell her—

Nah. Later.

"It'd be a shame to let this much mistletoe go to waste..."

She gives me a coy look. I waggle my eyebrows.

"Wow. You really are smarter than you look," she says, lips twitching.

"I know I should be offended, but I'm going to ignore your sass and kiss you now."

Pressing my lips to hers, I tell her without words everything I think about her. She's a brat (in the best way). She's funny. Beautiful. Precious. Brilliant.

She's worth adoring.

Worth everything.

We're a jumble of lips and hands, and I'm about to lose my mind with wanting when she rips her lips away with an exclamation. I grunt in protest, reaching for her.

"Oh my gosh, I'm sorry, but I really have to pee."

Not good. It's eight o'clock, maybe later, we have no phones, and no one's coming to look for us unless security is a Sherlock-level deductionist and figures out where to look simply by spotting Alessia's keys on the empty reception desk.

At the desperation in her eyes, I see it's time to be the man and get my woman what she needs.

Except I'm not dumb enough to attempt breaking down a solid door with my shoulder or foot. I work out, so strength isn't the concern. I could do it if I wanted, but why risk a broken bone over the holidays?

Work smarter, not harder.

Hmm. How does that play out here?

"Do you have a toolbox?" I ask, examining the lock.

This really is a nonsensical design.

"I remember seeing one when I reorganized. Hang on."

Alessia disappears around the corner of the L-shaped space and returns a minute later with a black, flat-bottomed canvas tool bag. It's perfectly organized, of course. I'd expect nothing less of her. Peering inside, I grab the easily accessible Phillips head screwdriver, and in minutes I've undone the two screws on the doorknob faceplate.

Less than a minute after, we're free.

Pride and satisfaction surge through me as I suck in a breath of fresh hallway air. I have an overwhelming urge to beat my chest like the alpha gorilla warding off the wimpy betas.

I'm the man.

"Yes, babe. You're the man." She pats my chest, grinning while shaking her head.

Oops. With a kiss to my cheek, she dodges past me through the door and down the hall toward the restrooms.

"I'll thank you better in a minute!" she yells.

I stare after her, all that testosterone going to waste in her absence.

One of the male residents catches me staring and raises an eyebrow. Shaking his head as he shuffles away, chuckling, I hear him mutter, "Sap."

My cheeks and neck heat, but my embarrassment is short-lived. I may be a sap, but at least I'm her sap. And that's enough.

Chapter 21

Alessia

I think I'm in love with Danger Stevens.

How is that possible? It hasn't been long enough.

Okay, so he's been part of my life for years, but I didn't love the guy at twelve. Or seventeen. Or any of the other years I wavered in my loathing to crush on him.

Now, though, I'm helpless. He's so stinking *lovable*.

I wish I could describe the way Dan looked when he removed the lock on the storage room door. Honestly, I half expected him to crow Peter Pan style. Or pump his arms and preen like the villains in every *Rocky* movie.

He's such a dork.

Then, so am I.

We're a couple of weirdos who, surprisingly, go together like Klara and Alfred in *The Shop Around the Corner* (a timeless classic far superior to its badly dated nineties re-envisioning). Lots of contention in the beginning, but once we had time to get to know each other... ah, chemistry.

Pressing the final piece of tape on the last package I had left to wrap this morning before needing to leave for the airport, I recline against my couch with a sigh and survey my work. I hope everyone is satisfied with my selections. Gift giving is the hardest love language to speak, at least for me. It doesn't help that I overthink it and psych myself out, which leads to procrastinating and suddenly having dozens of brilliant ideas that require more time than I have left. Inevitably, I wind up with hurried purchases which aren't horrible, just not as perfect as I wanted.

Oh well. Nothing I can do now. Christmas is this weekend.

Today I'm going to enjoy visiting with my sister and get her settled, then tomorrow is already booked up with final wedding details. Thank goodness Silas and Peggy opted to forego a rehearsal in lieu of spending more time with her kids and grandkids before the wedding. I'm looking forward to a few peaceful nights with my sister. And Dan if I can swing it.

Unless he wants to be with his own family, of course.

Will I be invited?

Is it too early in our relationship to do major holidays together?

Stop, brain.

I don't have the time or energy for another anxiety spiral.

Audrey hops over to sniff at my fingers, shoving her head under my relaxed palm. She's so cute, begging for pets. Happy to oblige, I relish the softness of her fur as I scratch her favorite spot between her ears right above her closed eyes. I run my hands down the length of her ears, and immediately feel more centered and relaxed.

The alarm on my phone startles us both. Time to pick up Paige.

Before she hops away, I scoop up my rabbit and take her outside to her hutch. "Come on, sweet girl."

A cold breeze whips through my sweatshirt and leggings. *Brr.* I add another few handfuls of bedding and hay before refilling her food and petting her one more time.

"It's supposed to fall below thirty tonight, so I'll bring you inside when I get home," I coo.

She thumps and dives into her burrow. I secure her hutch and cover it with an old moving blanket, lock up the house, and drive toward the airport.

Paige's flight is late. I circle the loop around the Albuquerque International Sunport three times before she texts to say she's at the curbside pickup lane. I spot her between numbered poles four and five and exhale. The tension that threatens to overwhelm me anytime I get near the airport (it's so confusing!) loosens further when there's ample room to pull close to the curb.

I climb out though I'm not supposed to, and security's probably going to yell at me to move in the next forty-five seconds, but I haven't seen my sister in six months. She's getting a hug. End of story.

Paige squeals after hoisting her carryon into my popped trunk and throws her arms around me. The scent of her signature vanilla sugar body spray is like getting hugged by a cookie. A tall, gorgeous, red-headed cookie.

She lets go first, holding me away from her while she studies my face as if she expects me to have changed drastically since July. I take a second to catalog any change in her, but she's as beautiful and effervescent as always.

Her eyes are an earthy brown-green framed by long, fake eyelashes I would blind myself attempting to apply—the same color as her mother's. She gets her height from her mother too. The only features we both inherited from Dad are our oval face shape, high cheekbones, and prominent Italian noses. We'll never be accused of being twins, but anyone who spends more than ten minutes with us can tell we're sisters.

"It's so good to see you!" she says.

I roll my eyes and stick out my tongue. She does the same, and now we both have the giggles.

"Move along!" The neon-vested airport security guy prods.

Still laughing, we climb into our seats and peel away from the curb. Having her next to me does my heart good. I've missed her.

"How was your flight?" I ask, and she launches into a story about a man giving her the heebie-jeebies when she got on the plane, inviting her to sit next to him. Luckily, a much cuter guy without any freaky vibes had a vacant seat next to him farther down the plane.

"So, when Zane asked for my number after we landed—" She sees my raised eyebrow and grins. "Don't worry, I gave him my @s instead. If he asks me out while I'm here..." She shrugs.

"Seriously, Paige? He could be a total creeper. Or married!"

"I checked. No indentation or tan line on his finger. Besides, it's only a date."

Paige and I have very different views on dating. As in, I rarely do, and she's always on the lookout for her next Mr. Right. Don't get me wrong, Paige is an intelligent young woman of faith with morals and impeccable standards, she just inherited Dad's natural charm and has no qualms with employing it at will.

You'd think it would bother me, but Paige's motivation is so counter to Dad's, they're barely in the same sphere.

"So..." she drags the syllable. "Tell me about Mr. Warning Label."

My mind scatters in a dozen different directions, each one of them flushing my face a new shade.

"Oh my gosh, you're blushing! What have you been keeping from me?"

I fill her in on the latest developments. We haven't had much time to talk, aside from random texts, since Dan and I went to Santa Fe. Her sighs, squeals, and *awws* at the right moments validate my feelings. Sometimes I get too in-my-own-head, and getting her perspective always helps me sort things out.

"I can't believe you didn't call me about any of this! I thought being sisters meant something." She crosses her arms and gives me a totally fake pout.

I take my eyes off the road long enough to show her how ridiculous I find her antics.

Paige breaks into a mischievous smile. "Don't roll your eyes at me, girlie. You're the one keeping secrets."

"I wasn't keeping secrets. You were wrapping up fall term and I've been busy at work! And, you know, getting stuck in closets with my boyfriend." Yes, I'm smiling too.

Paige sighs dreamily. "Stuck in a closet. Awesome trope."

"You're ridiculous." I shake my head, suppressing a smile.

"After all these years of waffling, detailing the reasons why Danger Stevens is the literal worst, you need to tell me some amazing bits to offset the bad."

"Fair enough," I concede, taking the interstate exit toward my house. I tell her about him putting lights on my house the other day. She beams, having listened to me whine about wanting them but never doing it myself year after year.

"Then, yesterday morning, Ms. Peggy was showing me her wedding dress. Side note—she made it herself with help from her daughter. Did I tell you she was a seamstress? Anyway, I went by the storage room afterward to clean up the mistletoe, but when I got there, the lock had been changed! I stopped by Maintenance to thank Luis, and he denied knowing anything about it."

"Oh, now that is sweet. So, Dan installed a new lock for you?"

"Yep, and it's a regular one-sided lock now. He made copies of the keys for the staff who might need one, too."

"Wow. The man's quite an overachiever."

"I know, right? Who needs grand gestures when you have acts of service?"

Paige scoffs. "Oh, no. I still want grand gestures. All of them. The grander, the better. Though, there is something to be said for the little things."

We reach our house, and I'm contemplating her words on the way inside. She begs off to take a quick shower before we head to dinner together as I weigh what she said about grand gestures.

I think she's wrong. If not objectively wrong, I feel wrong applying them to me. When I think about what drew me to Dan these past several weeks, I can't choose one big thing that changed my perception and helped me see *him*. It was several seemingly insignificant things added up to make me feel loved and want to love in return.

I've read about love languages. The concept of filling someone's tank is sensible. To me, a love tank isn't so different from the way our bodies need the right foods to be fueled. Yeah, you can eat a huge meal all at once and stuff yourself silly. But the best for a body is usually smaller, balanced, nutrient-dense meals.

I think love should be like that—showing the people you love how you feel, what they mean to you, in a myriad of ways, not a one-time over-the-top gesture.

But what do I know? I've never had much in the way of relationships outside of my dysfunctional family.

Paige is a sucker for romantic comedies and romance novels. She dates. Which makes her closer to expert than I'll ever be.

Except I can't deny the way Dan makes me feel. The peace I have when I'm with him that I don't around other people. The way his heated looks say I'm the most beautiful woman he's ever seen. The way he accepts me and my internal freakouts and monologues, puts up with my moodiness, and jumps in to help when he knows I'd never ask.

Personal gestures, individually tailored to me.

Maybe it's not love—yet—but it feels like we're on our way.

A loud bang followed by a pained moan yanks me out of my head and into the present.

"Paige?" I traipse down the hall to the spare bathroom and knock on the door. "Everything okay?"

She flings the door open, steam pluming past her into the hall. Clutching her towel tightly around herself, she grabs my arm and guides me to a seat on the closed toilet.

"You need to be sitting for this."

Uh oh. Her face is pale, and moisture gathers along her lower lashes. She sits on the edge of the tub and swallows before meeting my worried gaze.

"What's wrong, Paige? Just say it."

"Remember how I was concerned why Dad would want us both to come see him for Christmas?"

I think back to our conversation over Thanksgiving weekend and nod.

"Dad left a voicemail while I was in the shower. He knows we're spending the holiday together and said he needs to talk to us about something. Says it's important." She looks ready to burst into tears. "What if—" she sniffles, reaching for a tissue from the box on the edge of the sink. "What if it's bad? What if he's, like, dying?"

My mind spins, collecting and rejecting possibilities.

I can't stand to wait around until the fear of the unknown feeds off both of our corpses.

Yes, *I know* I watch too many movies. Judge me when I'm not worried about my dad, m'kay?

Ten seconds later, I get Dad on the line. I ask a few questions, then hang up.

"Paige, breathe. He says it's not life-threatening, but he's glad we're both here because he's flying in tomorrow at noon."

She blinks at me, her face a wash of confusion, and then lets loose the kind of belly laugh that only comes from relief.

"We're spending Christmas with Dad after all!"

I don't think it's funny in the least.

Chapter 22

Dan

It's Christmas Eve, and I can't wait to surprise Alessia.

I've got a secret I've been keeping from her for weeks.

At first, I was doing it to get a rise out of her. Full disclosure, it wasn't even me in the beginning. I kind of took over the role once I discovered how badly it irritated her. Thought it would be funny to mystify her, keep her guessing who the culprit was.

Of course, this was before we got distracted with her extensive activities calendar and crossing off wedding to-dos between dates and kissing sessions. I mean, how's a guy supposed to sneak around pulling pranks when he's spending all his time with the woman he's intent on pranking?

Don't worry, it's a good prank.

Well, I hope she'll see it that way eventually.

We had a delightful time with it in the storage room, after all. You have no idea how difficult it was not to spill the beans and confess right then and there. It would've been so simple.

Alessia, I'm the mistletoe mischief maker.

I've even got alliteration going for me.

Gauging by her reaction in the closet, I can't imagine she'll be too upset. She might be on board with my original plan to honor tradition beneath all those symbolic plastic sprigs.

I'm grinning like an idiot as I glance around the hallways furtively. Empty. *Excellent.* From my coat pocket, I retrieve an industrial stapler, flick the pin to open it flat, and staple the endpiece to the top of the doorframe between her office and the storage room. She's taken this one down the most often, so I get an extra rush of glee each time I put it back up. This time I added a festive red ribbon.

The prank was getting expensive, so I was happy to find she'd saved them for me. When I replaced the faulty lock on the closet, I stuffed my pockets and have been stealthily adhering them to every empty doorway since.

Childish? Probably.

Worth it? Absolutely.

A throat clears as I reach into my pocket for the last sprig, this one for the doorway between Pam's desk and the common area. It's the riskiest one so far, but I have it on good authority Alessia is busy with Silas and Peggy in the pool house, running through their ceremony one last time.

Dropping the stapler and mistletoe into my coat pockets, I clasp both hands behind my back and am tempted to whistle like the conspicuous doofus I am. Stealth has never been my forte.

The newcomer leans against the wall opposite me, smiling with a look of interest. She's tall and redheaded with hazel eyes brimming with mischief. I might've been intrigued were I not already head over heels for a certain average-height raven-haired beauty. (I read that in my Garrett Wilson novel last night and thought it an apt description for my Alley Cat.)

"Hi," she says in a husky tone.

"Hi," I reply hesitantly with a glance toward the lobby.

Alessia's spent too many years thinking I'm a skirt-chasing flirt. I'm not about to put myself in a position to prove her fears correct. No way.

"You're Danger Stevens." It's a statement, not a question.

Something in the shape of her face is familiar, but I've never met this woman before. I'd remember.

"I am."

Her eyes glimmer with mirth. Wow. She's gorgeous and knows it. It's in the purse of her lips, the way she's fighting a smile full of secrets. I'm growing more uncomfortable by the second. Until she extends her hand.

"I'm Paige."

My shoulders relax, and I allow myself to return her smile, albeit mine's more polite than anything else. She's got a decent handshake. Firm and self-assured.

"I've heard a lot about you from Als."

"*Als?* Interesting. I call her Les."

I shrug. "Als. Alley Cat. Sometimes Kitty."

"And she let you live? Wow, she really does like you now."

A laugh shoots past my lips.

"I see you've been busy," Paige smirks, nodding toward the offshoot hallways of the main building, each head jamb bearing a sprig of mistletoe. "Hedging your bets?"

"Not anymore," I grin. "Now it's just fun messing with her."

She laughs, throwing her head back similar to Alessia when she's really letting go. I see their familial resemblance now. It's faint, but apparent in the nose and cheekbones. I'm cataloguing mannerisms too.

"Can I help?" she asks.

"I suppose." I dig in my pockets and extract the final sprig and the stapler, handing both to her.

"You be lookout," she whispers, craning her neck toward each hallway.

Chuckling, I accept my duty and stay close in case I need to tug her out of sight. She's only an inch or so shorter than me, so with minimal effort she fastens the mistletoe in place and snaps the stapler closed with a smirk. Loads of mischief in those eyes.

Affection rises within me, much the way I feel when Tory gets an eerily similar glint—a look that's gotten me into more trouble than I can list. Heaven forbid the pair of them ever meets.

"Oh! Look," says an older woman I've never seen before. "You're under the mistletoe!"

My shoulders droop. Some lookout I am. How do I get us out of the precise situation I'd hoped to avoid?

Paige tugs at my coat pocket. I note the weight of the stapler as it drops inside. With a sly head nod of acknowledgment, I smile at the newcomer then look up.

"Huh. What do you know." I pretend to study the greenery as if I'm only now noticing it.

"You know what happens now!" The lady clasps her hands as if she's personally responsible for her perceived budding romance. "Go on, it's tradition."

"Oh," Paige says, shaking her head. "No. This is my brother."

The stranger gives her a skeptical look. "I didn't make the rules."

Paige's concerned gaze meets mine. I shrug, hoping if I comply the woman will leave, and we can find Alessia before she discovers what I've been up to.

"Cheek?" I ask, unwilling to make Paige uncomfortable no matter what tradition dictates.

At her nod, I lean in and press my lips to the edge of her cheek. It's over in a split second, but that fraction of time is precisely the moment Alessia enters.

"Really?" She says flatly, as if she's disappointed, yet expected something like this would happen.

"It's not how it looks," I insist, raising my hands as if the motion proves I wasn't touching anyone inappropriately.

It's stupid. I'm stupid. I should've told the lady no. Run away. Dang it.

"Les, it's not what you think," Paige adds.

"I should think not!" The harbinger of trouble cries wearing an expression of disgust. "He's *her brother*." She shakes her head and proceeds on her merry way unaware of the damage she's caused.

Alessia's eyebrow wings up. "Okay."

She glances at the clock on the wall opposite the reception desk. "Paige, we need to go now, or we'll be late."

"Go?" *Where? I want to ask. May I come?*

My gaze zeroes in on Alessia, trying to get a read on her, but her eyes are shuttered in a way I haven't seen before. This is bad. She's always been an open book with me, never hiding her disdain or, more recently, her affection.

I need to ensure this doesn't set us back. That she understands I would never make a move on her sister or anyone else now we're together. That I'm hers and always will be.

I blink. *Whoa, there, buddy.* Now is not the time for the admission of big feelings.

Alessia's eyes drift shut as if she, too, is having big thoughts and attempting to regain control. My stomach sinks. My chest feels like it's been punched by a giant fist.

"We'll talk later, okay?" She says, and I can't tell by her tone whether she means to reassure or accuse. "We have to go now, Paige."

Paige meets my terror-filled eyes. She mimes taking a deep breath and exhaling using hand motions, then mouths *I'll talk to her.* She takes long strides through the door and into the parking lot after Alessia.

I'm lost.

Then I'm disappointed. Beyond frustrated.

Alessia ought to know by now. I've proven myself over and over these past weeks.

I never did anything to make her doubt me in the first place. I'm not her father. Not even close.

She's chosen time and again to view me through a specific lens I never deserved, never earned. It stings.

More than stings. It crushes me.

Breathe.

Clenching my fists against the swift desire to take out my frustration on the nearest hunk of drywall, I instead storm out to my SUV and head to the gym. It's healthier to pray while working out my feelings than to hit things. First, I head through the drive-thru for tacos. My sisters' preferred emotional support foods were always brownies or ice cream. Me? I need spicy meat and cheese dripping with grease and sauce from either end of a crunchy corn shell.

Once my belly's full, my head has sorted itself out again. Lord willing, Alessia will hear me out after Paige tells her side. She'll know the truth and trust me. I'll keep showing her she can.

It's up to her to decide if she's brave enough to love me.

All I can do is love her either way.

Chapter 23

Alessia

"It was my cheek, Les. He didn't want to, but that lady was a pushy old bird," Paige says the second her butt hits the passenger seat.

Once she's buckled, I peel out of the lot as fast as I dare, careful to watch for pedestrians. We are so late.

"I know."

"You do? Then why are you upset?"

I take a moment to analyze my feelings.

Paige texted to let me know she'd arrived at Valle Encantado, having dropped me at work this morning so she could have my car while I put the finishing touches on the pool house before we had to leave to pick up Dad at the airport. I'd let her know it would be a few minutes while I put away my supplies and locked everything up for the holiday weekend.

As I walked the hall toward the front desk, I bemoaned the addition of several sprigs of mistletoe, but I didn't have the time or ambition to pull them down anymore. I heard what Mrs. Walker said, and Paige calling Dan her brother. I saw their unspoken conversation.

Intellectually, I know neither one of them wanted any part of Mrs. Walker's insistence on upholding tradition. Dan was both chivalrous and careful with the placement of his nanosecond lip press.

It was the look that got me—the conversation without words. I don't know why it stung, but it did. Immediately and without conscious will, my thoughts spiraled into wondering when they'd met, how they'd met, how long had they known one another to have such an intimacy. Silent conversations are for couples who've known one another so long they don't need words, right?

Their protests were unnecessary. I *knew* neither had been a willing participant. It wasn't even a real kiss. Dan hadn't put the moves on my sister, nor vice versa.

My hurt was irrational. I know that too.

Maybe it hit so hard because my nerves were already shot after a poor night's sleep spent tossing and turning over why Dad would leave his wife in Nashville behind for an impromptu holiday with us. Maybe it's that I've been increasingly aware of my feelings for Dan despite more than a decade and a half of resisting them. For so long, he's represented my deepest fears stemming from my dad's infidelity, and now both of those worlds are about to clash.

I've often wondered if telling Dad the truth about how his actions affected me would benefit my mental health or if it would simply put him on the defensive. He's never expressed regret for what he did, at least not to his two oldest daughters.

I can't speak for the others since I've never really known them.

"Les? *Please* talk to me," Paige begs. Her tone drips with misery.

I tug my gaze from the interstate ahead and glance at my sister to find her brows slanted downward and lips pinched in worry. I cringe, hating the way I got lost in my head again and left her hanging.

"I'm okay. Promise. I trust you and, shockingly, I trust Dan."

Feels right to say so aloud, and it's true. I *do* trust him. More than I knew even an hour ago. Dan would never willingly hurt me. I don't know *how* I know, I just do, and that fills me with peace enough to put aside the twinge of anxiety and hurt I felt when I saw their shared look under the mistletoe.

"Then help me understand what's going on in your head."

I shrug and toss her a grimace. "I've got issues. Dad's betrayal really messed me up, you know?"

She nods. "Same."

If anyone understands, it's her.

I was twelve when my world imploded at the revelation of her existence. She was seven. Quiet, observant, and too mature for her age. We forged a tenuous relationship once I got over my resentment toward her, which didn't last as long as you might expect, considering the impact the situation itself still has on me. I'd always wanted a sibling, and she treated me with such hero worship I couldn't shield my heart from her if I tried. The circumstances of her birth weren't her fault—they were Dad's.

Once I retargeted my anger to the party truly responsible, forging a long-distance sisterhood was easy. Dad arranged with both our moms to overlap our visitation schedules and holidays. We grew closer as she entered high school, the same time I began distancing myself from Mom in college. Paige graduated high school and did her undergrad here in Albuquerque. As roommates our relationship grew from sisterhood to friendship, and it felt as though a part of me was amputated when she moved to California for law school.

Paige knows me better than anyone, so it shouldn't surprise me when she pokes me in the arm and says, "You're in love with him, aren't you?"

"N—" There's no point denying I have feelings, but love? I still haven't decided for sure. "Maybe?"

Paige laughs. "Gotcha. Word of advice? Figure it out and tell him sooner rather than later. He looked pretty shaken up when you stormed out."

"I didn't storm out."

"Yeah, you did."

Groaning, I take the exit toward the arrivals level at the Sunport for the second time this week. Paige gets a text from Dad letting us know where he's waiting, and it's time to push thoughts of Danger Stevens and my feelings for him aside.

I'm going to need all my emotional resources to deal with whatever prompted Dad to drop everything and fly to Albuquerque for Christmas.

"Does my heart good to see you girls together," Dad says with a happy smile as we enjoy our Christmas Eve dinner of Dino's pepperoni and green chile pizza in my living room.

I say happy, but there are shadows behind his eyes I study with growing concern. He's trying hard to act like nothing's wrong, so I'll give him a pass until after dinner.

He reaches across my coffee table for another slice. "I've missed this."

"The pizza?" Paige snickers around a mouthful.

"That too, but I mean the three of us enjoying a meal like old times. Pizza straight from the box in the living room, good music in the background. Though, your house is way nicer than some of the places I lived then."

"Thanks, Dad." I accept the compliment without reading anything into it.

Dad always made enough money to avoid the starving artist stereotype, though some years not by much. Now that I'm older and more cynical, I wonder how much of his income went into supporting his assorted offspring.

As far as I know, Paige and I are the only two kids he has much of a relationship with. Paige has tried harder to get to know our other half-siblings than I have, which I suppose is logical since Dad and her mom's affair only lasted a couple of years. Paige never really had a nuclear family with two married parents the way I did, so she didn't need therapy to process her world upending as mine had.

By the time we learned there were more kids out there, I was in high school. Life was contentious enough with Dad by then, so I avoided him unless Paige was around. Not much has changed.

Dad and Paige are on their feet clearing the dinner detritus when I realize I've been in my head again. Paige won't think anything of it, but if I know Dad, he'll have some remark about my rudeness or how closed off I am.

Surprisingly, he doesn't say a word, but as the evening fades with the setting sun, Dad's mood follows.

Paige and I shoot each other concerned looks. She hasn't missed his weird vibes either. His calling to ask us to spend Christmas with him in Nashville was weird enough, but showing up with twenty-four hours' notice and no explanation is so far out of character for him, we're more than a little concerned.

"Is everything okay, Dad?"

I breathe a grateful sigh Paige was brave enough to broach the subject first.

Dad's fingers tap a beat on his knee as his heel bounces a counterrhythm.

"Please, Dad," I urge, twisting my fingers in my lap. "Paige is worried you're sick or something. If it's bad news, please tell us."

"I'm healthy as far as I know. I—" He shoves his fingers into his hair, still naturally dark and barely graying along his temples. "I just didn't want to spend Christmas alone."

His admission has Paige and I consulting each other in silence over the top of his bent head.

"What about Cherise?"

"Chelsea," Paige corrects under her breath.

Whoops.

"Sorry. *Chelsea.* It's your first Christmas."

"She kicked me out."

My mind's whirling, none of the thoughts helpful or beneficial.

"What happened, Dad?"

Thank God for Paige.

"She's been having an affair from the start," he says after several long moments. "I'd just signed on with White Hellebore when we met. Knew we'd be on the road; said she was okay with it. Our love was strong enough, absence makes the heart grow fonder, blah blah blah. Same"—curse—"I used to tell women when I wanted to keep them on the hook. But I was such a fool in love I didn't see her using my own tactics."

Wow. Didn't see that one coming. They looked so happy at their wedding in January. Admittedly, I didn't exactly spend much time getting to know the woman, but she looked at him with stars in her eyes and he as if she hung the moon. All the clichés.

"I found out in August. I was wrecked, but not ready to throw in the towel. Begged her to do counseling, agreed to an open marriage, whatever she needed."

"Dad, that's not—"

"I know it's not healthy, okay?" he says, in a voice so broken I'm fighting compassionate tears I never imagined having for this man. "But I love her."

Paige scoots closer to Dad on the couch and puts her arm around him. She's always been so much better at handling emotions. He starts crying, and it guts me so hard I'm ready to join him. Men's tears always get to me, and I've never seen my dad cry.

There's not much room on the other side of Dad, but I squeeze into the spot. He and Paige shift to create space, and the three of us sit there a long time as Dad explains how she kicked him out the same day the band let him go to reinstate their original guitarist. I want to find the fair-weathered opportunistic gold-digger he married and rip her hair out.

At the same time, a tiny piece of me buried way deep-down murmurs, "what goes around, comes around." Am I a horrible person? I don't want to hear those words, and I'm working toward silencing them.

Forgiveness is an ongoing process, I hear.

Dad stares at his crisscrossed hands resting on spread knees. "How many people have I hurt?" I cringe as he misuses the Lord's name. "I'm so sorry I hurt you both. You two are the best parts of me. I've spent my whole—" cursing "—life being an—" ugly word. "No more. You deserve better."

The rest of the night is surreal. Once Dad finishes pouring his heart out under Paige's patient consolation, he gets up as though nothing happened. Not in a way that suggests he's disingenuous, more like how I separate my feelings sometimes into buckets to better focus and not let any single emotion take over. It's weird to observe the behavior in someone else, but knowing we share genes, it's comforting in a way to recognize a similarity between me and my dad. I've never really looked for any, aside from physical attributes.

The three of us end up having a wonderful Christmas Eve. Dad and Paige sing carols, their voices harmonizing beautifully. I have mercy on them, mouthing the words instead of subjecting them to my goose honk. We follow the city's luminaria tour through the country club area, and though we're stuck in slow moving, bumper to bumper traffic the entire time, it gives us plenty of opportunities to catch Dad up on our lives. For the first time, I think he's truly listening... and possibly cares more than I've given him credit for.

I crawl into bed late, my heart and head full to the brim. It's been quite the day, and I'm going to be up for hours processing everything.

One thing can't wait, though.

I call Dan to clear the air. He doesn't answer, so I send him a brief text, hoping if he's already asleep he'll see it in the morning.

I'M SORRY. I DO TRUST YOU. PLEASE CALL ME.

When fifteen minutes pass without a response, I send one more message in case he's not asleep. I shouldn't. I ought to give it to God and trust Dan will reply tomorrow, but I can't. I type three simple words that convey the churning feelings I'm wrestling with instead of sleeping.

ARE WE OKAY?

I don't remember falling asleep, but when I wake in the morning, my text shows as read.

No reply.

What have I done?

Chapter 24

Dan

Christmas Day dawns early and far too loud.

After last night's much-needed Christmas Eve service, Rick, Scout, and the kids slept over as is our tradition, and judging by the scuffle I hear, the munchkins are already awake. Scout shushes them, but they'll only be able to contain the beasts so long.

I get out of bed, yawning and stretching, and plod to the Jack-and-Jill bathroom I've shared with Tory since childhood. Mom doesn't care about my perfectly nice house across the street with a real bed instead of a futon in the corner of Mave's new nursery. The whole family wakes up on Christmas morning under the same roof. End of story.

Tory barges in the second I finish essential ablutions—no one's allowed to shower or dress either—and grumbles about renting a place in Rio Rancho. It's an empty threat. We both know moving twenty minutes away isn't going to get her out of sharing a bathroom with me on Christmas morning.

I chuckle as I close myself into my former bedroom to change my underwear and put on a T-shirt. Mom can force us to wear our pajamas, but I haven't slept in a shirt since I was a kid, and I refuse to spend half the day in yesterday's briefs. Before heading downstairs, I take my phone off the charger and reread Alessia's messages from last night.

She called in the middle of the candlelight service, but by the time we returned home it was too late to call her back. Much as I wanted to reply to her texts, I didn't know what to say. I'm relieved she texted me, but she left me wondering the entire day.

If she cares about me, why would she do that?

I've been ready to go all-in from the beginning, and I know she needs to process longer than most and often gets stuck in her own head, but man. Sometimes I'm left wondering if she and I are in the same book, let alone on the same page. I'm in a holiday romance while she's over in a psychology journal.

My head is pounding. I need coffee before anything else.

Grams is in the kitchen when I walk in, pulling out a tray of her once-a-year cinnamon buns. They're not quite as good as the craft fair lady's, but they're still delicious.

"Smells amazing, Grams."

"Thanks, Danny. Bacon or sausage?" Grams points her spatula to the cast iron skillet on the stove.

"Both. Coffee?" I yawn, scratching my stomach.

"Pot's on. There's plain vanilla or Tory's fancy peppermint creamer in the fridge."

Peppermint reminds me of Alessia. I choose the vanilla.

I need to reply to her texts, but I'm tied between wanting to show up at her place and obligation to my family. I wish we could've figured everything out yesterday and then spent Christmas Eve together, side by side in the worship service before heading to my house to argue over another sappy Christmas movie. With Paige in town, that was never going to happen, but a guy can dream.

The rest of the clan traipses in and out of the kitchen, filling plates with food, glasses with juice, or mugs with coffee, then taking seats around the long dining room table we use when everyone's here and it's too cold to eat al fresco. Normally, I relish the kids' antics, my sisters and their husbands' teasing, and the sheer volume of noise we create. *Husband* this year. Brian's loss is written in the shadows of everyone's expressions.

My gaze assesses Mave, a habit I've developed over these past months. She appears to be doing all right, but I worry about her. I can only imagine the grief of losing a spouse, so I have no way to gauge what's normal and what isn't. She cried last night during the service, and I heard the soft murmurs of her and Tory's voices late into the night on the other side of the bathroom door, so I know she's letting herself feel what she needs to feel. That's good.

But I worry she's putting on a brave face for the rest of us this morning.

After breakfast, Rick and I clear the table—another of Mom's rules is men clean up if the women cook and vice versa. By fifteen, I learned to cook simply to get out of seven days a week of dish duty.

We exchange gifts, laughing and teasing as always, and I'd almost believe it were a normal year and Brian's simply out of town if it weren't for Scout's big mouth.

From the guilt in her downturned expression, she didn't mean to say his name, an unspoken rule we'd been abiding by, but it's enough to change the atmosphere and break Mave. Scout races to Mave's side, wrapping her into a hug, as Mave's gasping sobs bring us to the verge of adding our own tears to the mix.

"I'm so sorry," Scout croons over and over as they rock together.

"No, I'm glad you said his name," Mave sniffles as they break apart. "To be honest, I was afraid to because I could tell you guys were trying so hard. I miss him so much, and I knew this first Christmas without him would be awful. But I'm not going to break if we talk about him."

Mave's gaze circles the silent room, watery but smiling. "I love you all. Thank you for surrounding me with love and family the past six months. I couldn't have faced it without any of you." She sniffs. "But do me a favor and quit treating me like I'll fall apart if you bring him up. He was my husband, he's gone, and I'm sad. But we had six wonderful years together," she pauses to run a hand lovingly over the enormous swell of her ready-to-pop belly. "And I want our baby to know everything about his or her daddy. Which means you'll need to tell him or her as many stories as I do."

Mom strides across the room and sits on the other side of Mave, folding her in a hug and patting Scout's shoulder at the same time.

Mave laughs a wet chuckle, wiping her eyes and nose with a tissue from the box I offer. "Now, thank you, but can we get back to our regularly scheduled Christmas gift exchange? I think somebody here is in a hurry to go see his sweetheart."

All eyes follow the direction of her gaze. Mine go wide at her pointed look. There's no hiding anything from this houseful of women too insightful for their own good, so I nod.

"Yes, where is she?" Mom asks.

"Would've thought you'd invite her." Grams adds.

My sisters wear knowing smirks, so I rise to my feet.

"You know what? You're absolutely right. I'll go remedy the situation right now." My glare dares them to challenge me.

"But Unca Dan, I want my last pwesent!" cries Zack, clutching a wrapped rectangular package.

The rest of the family laughs as he stomps his foot, putting both hands on his hips and frowning.

"Don't yaugh at me!"

Obediently, I press my lips together and screw my face into a serious expression as I resume my seat. "Apologies, little man. Proceed."

He wastes no time tearing into the box and crying out with delight at the Lego Duplo set. I can't wait till he's old enough to build with the regular sized ones. I'm going to have so much fun with them building my old Lego sets up in Grams's attic.

I leave Rick to present his final gift to Scout, a trip to Scotland I already know about, and sneak toward the front door. I catch Mom's raised eyebrow and mouth *Alessia*. She nods, giving permission for me to leave. Grabbing my keys, wallet, and phone from the bowl on the table at the foot of the stairs, I jog across the street, wincing at the cold seeping through my socked feet.

If I change quickly, I should be at her house in twenty minutes tops. Except when I look up, there's a car in my driveway. *Hers.*

It's off but still warm. A glance toward my front porch reveals Alessia bundled inside a heavy coat, hat, gloves, and boots as if we lived four hundred miles farther north instead of the Southwest desert. The sight of her sitting on the heavy oak bench Silas left behind flips my stomach. She's so beautiful it physically hurts to look at her, not knowing whether we're going to get past her issues or not.

"Hey," I say. Her being here is a good sign, right?

She gives me a smile I can't quite read. "Hi. I wasn't sure what to do when you weren't home."

I thumb toward Mom and Grams's house. Alessia nods.

Making quick work of the front deadbolt, I usher her into the warmth of my living room.

"Tea?" I offer, knowing how she hates coffee.

"Yes, please."

She lags a few steps behind, I'm guessing to shed her bulky outerwear, as I stride into the kitchen to fill a mug with water. I place it in the microwave to heat up and dig through the cabinet for the box of assorted herbal teas I bought purely for her. She selects one, and when the microwave beeps, retrieves the steaming mug, and drops the bag inside.

I enjoy the silence with Alessia as we return to the living room and take our seats on opposing ends of the couch same as we did on *Blue Hawaii* night. I've learned from countless conversations with my sisters to respect the time a woman needs to gather her thoughts.

She sips from her mug, stealing glances at me when she thinks I'm not looking. I pretend to examine my bookcases, keeping her in my periphery. Waiting.

"I'm sorry," she says eventually, setting her empty mug on the end table beside her. "Paige insists I stormed out yesterday, that you probably think I freaked out about the mistletoe kiss."

I say nothing but dip my head.

"I was laser focused on leaving to pick up my dad from the airport. Plus," Alessia sucks in a breath before continuing, her words spewing with increasing speed. "I found mistletoe everywhere and I didn't have time to take it down, and whoever keeps putting it up is driving me insane! Then I walk in and see my beautiful sister being kissed by the man I l–*like*—"

Her chest heaves after that episode of verbal vomit.

"I didn't—" She cuts me off with a hand raise.

"I know, Dan." She knows how much I love the way she says my name. Her gaze connects with mine, soft and open as she reaches her hand across the middle cushion. A silent invitation to meet halfway. "I didn't doubt you for a second. You are not the man I used to accuse you of being. I haven't believed that for a while. *I know you.* I know Paige. More importantly, *I trust you.*"

"Then why did you sound so annoyed? The way you glared at us and said, 'Really?' gave me chills." I shudder to prove my point.

She laughs softly through her nose. "Can I be honest? For a second there, I thought you or Paige were my mistletoe culprits. Silly, right?"

I bite back my own laugh, ready to confess, but she keeps talking.

"There was a look passed between the two of you, a secret sort of look, and I wondered if you knew each other somehow, and I don't know. It struck me as intimate, and I was jealous."

I scoot closer to her side of the couch. She studies the movement, tensing up until I reach for her hand. Her body melts into my touch as I scoot right up next to her until our thighs align and wrap my fingers around hers. My other hand glides up her arm, past her neck, to cradle her jaw.

"Thank you for telling me. Trusting me. I didn't know Paige until about three minutes before when she introduced herself. I was planning to ask you to lunch. Didn't know your dad was coming to town."

I'll be honest. It hurt she hadn't shared her Christmas plans. We'd talked about spending the holiday with my family and inviting Paige once she confirmed her flight plans.

"I'm sorry," Alessia says, pressing her cheek into my palm like a cat. My Alley Cat.

The thought prompts a smile.

She explains about her dad's vague voicemail which sent Paige into a panic. "If I hadn't called to clarify, he would've shown up completely unannounced."

"How'd it go?" I hate the way my frustration and her laser focus kept us apart last night.

"Amazing," she says with a peaceful sigh, then proceeds to run through the evening's events and revelations in detail. "It was one of the best Christmas Eves in years."

"That's awesome."

Her free hand traces gentle figure eights on the back of our clasped hands. She'll lull me to sleep if she keeps it up. "Hey, I was wondering something."

"Mm-hmm?" I murmur, half catatonic now.

"How come you never talk about your dad?"

I shrug. "Never knew him. He disappeared shortly after I was born, then later Mom learned he died. No one really talked about the details, and it became this undiscussed *thing* lurking in the background. I asked Tory once, but she didn't know. Scout and Mave told us stories from when they were really little, but by then their memories had faded too much to glean any real feelings."

Mom is not the kind of woman to discuss what she doesn't want to, and I've never wanted to push her into a subject that might cause her pain.

"That's sad," she says.

I shift to make room for her in the circle of my arms. She gladly shimmies into position as I lean into the corner, adjusting until we're mostly horizontal along the length of the couch.

"It is what it is. I had a huge family of women who loved me, and then I had Silas."

"And now you have me." She presses a kiss to my chest through my shirt. I kiss the top of her head.

"Do I?" I'm pathetic for asking, but I need to know where we stand.

"Of course, you do. I'm so sorry for making you worry yesterday. You haven't given me a single reason to doubt you."

"And I never will," I say darkly, remembering there's one other story I need to tell her. "Cheating is one of the worst things you can do to a person whether the relationship is serious or not. It's still a betrayal and trusting someone again after is a huge risk."

"Is this what you've avoided telling me? The real reason you moved home?" Alessia's always had keen intuition.

I nod, clearing my throat and focusing on a deep breath in then out. "Her name was Santana, and she was the headmaster's daughter."

Alessia groans. "Not another cheesy trope. You're killing me, Smalls."

I chuckle at her *Sandlot* reference.

"You sure know a lot about tropes for someone who hates to read."

"Film studies, remember? Tropes are in movies too. Pretty sure *boss's daughter* is geared more toward the spicy romance crowd, regardless of format, though."

"Not mine, I assure you."

"Noted," Alessia says, wiggling to get comfortable. "Go on."

She's killing me with those wiggles.

Concentrate, man.

"We dated a few months, casually but exclusively, or so I thought. When I discovered she was also dating one of the high school science teachers, I tried to end it."

"Tried?" Alessia rolls onto her side, leaning back to study my face.

I shrug and fix my gaze to the ceiling. This woman is entirely too distracting.

"Santana didn't care for being dumped any more than she liked being faithful. For the rest of the school year, she circulated rumors, played up the drama for sympathy. Demanded I take her back, and when I refused, went crying to Daddy enough times he opted to let my contract expire."

"What about the other guy?"

"Heard they got married after the term ended. He landed an associate dean position at the recommendation of her father."

"And you landed back home."

"Precisely."

Alessia shakes her head against my shoulder. "I'm going to call her *Satana* in my head from now on. Devil-woman didn't deserve you."

Gosh, I love her. Laughing, I tug her into a tight embrace until she squeals and pinches my side.

Making my fingers into a claw shape, I tickle her until she gasps, squealing into a fit of giggles. Then I make her squirm by rubbing my facial hair into the sensitive skin along her neck.

"Release me, you oaf!"

I obey, laughing my head off when she gasps as her butt hits the floor. Her look of surprise is almost as adorable as her lost-in-thought face.

I'm dying to kiss her again, to tell her how I feel. For now, I let the heat in my gaze do the talking. She rises to her knees, mirroring my look with enough heat of her own to melt the Taos Ski Area.

Before I'm tempted to drag her back onto the couch, I put my hands on her shoulders. "Wait."

Her brow arches, but she complies.

"I want to tell you something, but first, open your Christmas present."

She makes an *aww* sound in her throat before she smiles. "Okay. I forgot yours at my house. Can I give it to you tomorrow?"

"Of course," I say, dropping to my knees to crawl under the tree for the flat, rectangular box.

"Oof," she grunts as I place it onto her lap. "It's heavy!"

In quick movements, she unwraps the box and peels off the lid. Her grin widens as she scans the contents and rolls her eyes.

My grin's similarly broad as she lifts the book from its tissue paper nest. "*Cinema is a Cat: a Cat Lover's Introduction to Film Studies*. You've got to be kidding me."

"I think you mean you've got to be *kitten* me." I pump my eyebrows. I'm a word guy. Puns are life.

"I love you," she says mid-eyeroll, shaking her head with a smile.

Surprise and warmth flow over me at her words. *God, if you love me, please let her mean them.*

"I love *you*," I echo sincerely.

She stills, and I watch the movement of her eyes as she replays the last ten seconds in her mind. Her gaze lands on mine as her cheeks go pink.

"You do?"

"Yes, Alessia. I love you." I search through the tissue paper in her gift box for her other gift. "Part of me has loved you since sixth grade social studies when you spearheaded our final project and said you were glad it wasn't science class because having *Danger* in the group was a bad omen."

She blushes hard. "I was so mean to you. I think I'm going to be apologizing to you for the next fifty years."

"Hurt people hurt people. I never took it personally." I kiss the side of her head.

She turns at the last second and catches my lips. "I love you too," she mumbles against my mouth before drawing me into a longer, more satisfying kiss.

As we break apart to catch our breath, I add, "Also, I'm happy to accept your apologies for the next fifty years. Especially if they're like this."

I unfold the tissue square in my hand to reveal a silver chain with a dangling cat silhouette charm.

Alessia scoffs, grinning with mischief. It's my new favorite expression. As soon as I've fastened the chain around her lovely neck, she goes in for another kiss. Instead, her fingers dive into my sides where it tickles the most. I squirm, dodge, and wriggle until I'm able to overpower her with a few well-placed tickles of my own.

Hovering over her as our panting breaths mingle, I still at the seriousness in her brown eyes. Seriousness *and* humor. It's a delightful combination.

"Danger? I'm sorry, but you need to kiss me right *meow*."

This is my life now. Fifty years of cat puns, movie analysis, laughter, tickle wars, and kissing the woman who loathed me until she got to know me.

I'm a smart man, so after sharing another laugh, I happily kiss her *right meow*. Thoroughly.

Chapter 25

Alessia

Monday morning, I take extra care with my appearance. My long, dark hair hangs in loose, glossy curls, a look I know Dan is especially fond of. Paige helps me with my eye makeup since I've never been able to do more than mascara without looking like the AI-generated offspring of a Kardashian and a clown.

"Done. You look amazing." Paige gestures a chef's kiss, gathering her eye shadow brushes and setting them into her makeup bag.

Compliments are tricky, and sometimes I forget to respond because I'm caught up debating too long between accepting the comment and waving it away. I manage to thank Paige and smile.

I step into a pale green floral print maxi dress with darker green leaves and red and pink flowers. It's a perfect mix of Hawaii and Christmas. I'll be freezing beneath my coat until I get in the building, of course, but it'll be worth a few shivers when I get to see Dan's reaction.

As I enter the living room with my coat over one arm and shoes in hand, Dad releases a low whistle.

"Lessi, *mia bellisima figlia.*"

My face warms at being called his beautiful daughter. Dad's primary use of Italian to make women swoon used to irritate me as a teenager, but today it reminds me of the way Nonno called me "*mia gioia.*" His joy. Emotion pours over me, and I'm terrified I'll ruin my makeup if I let myself get too sentimental.

Time to compartmentalize and focus on the task at hand: ensuring a flawlessly executed wedding day for two of my favorite seniors. After I accept Dad's compliment.

"*Grazie, Papino.*"

"Is Paige almost ready?" Dad asks, peering down the hall toward her bedroom.

"She'll be out any minute."

They're coming with me to the wedding. When Ms. Peggy learned I had family in town, she insisted. I wasn't about to refuse time with either of them when we have precious little left before they return to their homes at opposite ends of the country. Especially now that Dad and I are making more of an effort to mend our relationship.

I'm nervous to introduce Dan and his family to mine. It's early in our relationship to meet the parents, isn't it? I've met his whole family, but that was unintentional.

Dad has never met anyone I've dated, but then, Mom and Gerald haven't either. Which is in part because I was never in a relationship serious enough to reach this stage, but also because I've never believed they cared. Perhaps it's time to change that.

"Let's go, people!" Paige calls out, doing an exaggerated runway model strut, showing off her vintage style tea-length dress with a flared skirt and pineapple print, paired with sheer black tights and strappy white heels. Gorgeous as always.

Dad lets out a whistle for her, too, which brightens Paige's smile considerably. "*Oggi sei bellissima, mia cara.*"

"Thanks, Dad. I do look lovely, don't I?"

"You're going to freeze," Dad chuckles, holding out Paige's coat for her.

She slips her arms into the sleeves then bends over, pulling at her tights. "Nope, they only look sheer. They're skin-toned beneath the black and fleece-lined."

"Genius." Dad's smile matches mine.

I wish I had a pair. Cold and I do not get along. Luckily, the wedding is in the pool house, which is humid and warm year round, and I'll be too busy overseeing things to get cold. I only pray my hair doesn't frizz.

Paige breathes out a long, "wow," when I unlock the doors to the pool house, and we step inside.

"This is incredible," Dad agrees.

I am proud of how the room turned out. The space already lent itself well to a tropical theme with a freeform-shaped pool taking up just over a quarter of the space. It's rimmed with natural looking stacked boulders which serve as foundation to a small waterfall in the corner surrounded by potted ferns and palms. Large windows let in natural light.

The other corner is usually filled with lounge chairs surrounding the hot tub, but we moved them to storage for today. I didn't want anything out of place. The pool lifts blend in nicely thanks to their stone color, and the potted plants I placed in the chairs camouflage them further.

Previously bare beige walls are now papered along the bottom third with a roll of tall faux grass. I hauled in every single potted tree, real and fake, from the public areas around the community, and then strung dozens of garlands along the upper walls and parts of the ceiling to create a jungle effect. I even found faux tropical plants online with authentic looking flowers.

Dan helped me unbox the online deliveries of additional greenery, but he hasn't seen the final product. No one has but Peggy, who burst into happy tears Saturday morning when I did my preliminary reveal. I worked hard to keep it tasteful and avoided anything that might come off as tacky. Peggy and Silas deserve a beautiful wedding even if their theme still leaves me scratching my head.

My phone chimes with a text from Pam telling me the florist is here. I leave Dad and Paige in the pool house with the heavy roll of white anti-skid aisle runner and instructions for where to unfurl it. Once the flower arrangements arrive, I'll place them around the room to complete the island effect.

I'm beginning to sweat by the time I spot Dan heading toward the pool house through the large windows on the east wall, so I race to the locker room for a quick peek in the mirror. Thank goodness nothing is out of place or frizzy.

The double doors swing open as I reenter from the opposite side. Dan stills in the entry, his gaze drinking me in from head to toe. His perusal sends me into a full body flush. With long, determined strides, he crosses the room, gathers me into his arms, and dips me into a kiss reminiscent of Silas's smooth move at last week's game night.

"Goodness," I say. "That was some kiss."

Dan grins. "You look amazing. Seriously, wow."

"Thank you. So do you." *Boy, does he.*

Silas and Peggy asked guests to dress for the theme, but I never expected to find a Hawaiian shirt and linen pants so sexy.

My dad clears his throat from a few feet away. Dan turns, and I watch with a twitch at the corner of my lips as the pair take each other in.

"You must be Mr. Catano," Dan says, extending his hand. "I'm Dan."

Dad accepts his handshake, clapping Dan on the back before releasing him. "Vic. Heard a lot about you."

Dan smirks, sending me a sly wink which causes me to blush furiously. "Oh, really?"

"Actually, no." Dad says, clearly teasing. "Alessia has said virtually nothing. Who are you again?"

This is so weird, but I love it. Happiness bubbles inside until I feel like dancing and twirling over every surface. I wonder if I can persuade Dan to join me in recreating the "A Lovely Night" scene from *La La Land*. It fits the dynamic of our relationship so well.

The alarm on my phone jars me back into focus mode.

"The wedding's in half an hour!" I spring into action, directing Dan, Paige, and my dad as we straighten chairs and tweak the setup, then I excuse myself. Slipping into my coat, I hop into a golf cart and drive to the main building, then jog to the dining room kitchen to see how everything is coming there. The chef has it well in hand, and I have a wedding to get to.

On the way back, my mother calls.

"Hey, Mom," I answer.

"Merry Christmas, Alessia." She's a day late, but I'm not surprised. I didn't bother to call her, either.

"Merry Christmas. How was your holiday?"

She updates me on the kids and Gerald, and I smile at how happy she sounds.

"I missed you," she says, which does surprise me.

Christmas must be making everyone sentimental this year.

"I missed you too. And the kids." I plan to stop by later this week to give them their gifts.

She doesn't ask how I'm doing, but she does ask if I'll consider joining them for dinner on New Year's Eve. I accept on the condition I bring my boyfriend. Mom pauses but accepts.

The whole conversation lasts less than five minutes, but it's enough. Our relationship is what it is. Sure, I wish things were different, but I hope we'll have the chance to fix it the way I'm beginning to with Dad.

My next alarm rings when I'm halfway back to the pool house.

It's wedding time.

I duck into the seat Dan saved for me on the aisle. He threads our fingers together and kisses my temple. I close my eyes and savor the feel of his lips on my skin. I've never had a date at a wedding before. It's nice.

At the head of the packed room, Silas stands proud and handsome in his white tuxedo. Though, I'm not a fan of the large red lei around his neck as his nod to *Blue Hawaii*. Beside him centered under the floral arch, Pastor Johns is wearing the borrowed Elvis costume. It's silly but wonderful, and Silas looks so happy I might cry.

A shiver of excitement cuts through the room as the music cues Peggy's entrance. Dan squeezes my hand.

All heads turn as the bride enters the room on her son's arm. Her lilac-colored dress, embroidered with a border of white hibiscus, is a stunning homage to Joan Blackman's gown from the film's final scene. With her shoulder-length white hair curled into 1960s style waves, she could be a Golden Age movie star.

I sneak a glance at Silas. His eyes are rimmed, watery with emotion as he watches his bride glide toward him. In my periphery, Dan's as affected as I am. Resting my head against his shoulder, I exhale a million pent up emotions.

Peggy shared a bit of their story with me the other day. Learning how their love was torn apart by pride, family obligation, and the Vietnam war layers this day with significance. It's no wonder Silas is so emotional.

Peggy's gaze hasn't left Silas's since her feet hit the aisle runner. Her son Peter walks tall and proud beside her. The pair beams at me and Dan as they pass our row. When they reach Silas, the kiss and hug Peter bestows on his mother before he places her hand in Silas's has the whole assembly sniffling.

Pastor Johns breaks the ice with a ridiculously over-the-top Elvis impression, then guides Peggy and Silas through the standard vows before giving them the floor to add their own.

"You broke my heart at eighteen. I never wanted my family's money, nor the obligations that came with it. I only wanted you. It took me a long time to forgive you, Silas," Peggy says, her voice strong and sure. "In time, though, I came to understand why you wouldn't elope when my parents forbade our marriage. You never wanted to come between me and my family. Your sacrifice, though it pained me, gave me the courage to stand on my own two feet and eventually repair my relationship with them."

My eyes start to sting as I transpose my own family history onto Peggy's. It hits hard how much I want a better story for me and my parents than the one we've been creating. *Lord, I'm going to need Your help.*

Silas clears his throat and picks up their story. "Leaving you was the hardest choice I ever made. The horrors of war didn't compare to the pain of being separated from you. I came back a changed man, but I never forgot the love we shared. Never blamed you for marrying someone else. So long as you were happy, I could move on."

Peggy sniffles. Silas cups her jaw with his shaking hand, and I'm not sure how much longer I can hold in the tears.

"Except I never did move on," Silas admits with a chuckle. "More than sixty years later, you still take my breath away. My heart did little more than keep me alive until that August day when you smiled at me, and it started beating again. I will love you until it stops beating and I take my first breath in Heaven."

"And I will love you the same, Silas Cooper," Peggy adds. "All my days belong to you until the Lord calls us home."

Pastor Johns leads a short prayer and pronounces them husband and wife. Silas wastes no time in kissing his bride, dipping her in a film-worthy kiss that has everyone laughing and applauding. They face the crowd, joined hands lifted high in the air. I don't know who starts the cheering, but it ripples down the rows as the happy couple marches past.

I want a love able to survive a sixty-year separation and bring a roomful of people to tears.

Dan leans forward before standing and meets my gaze.

Scratch that.

I want a love that doesn't need to survive a separation.

A love that lasts sixty years through misunderstandings, apologies, and ridiculous arguments over movies. A love that comforts, reassures, accepts without judgment. A love that builds up, teases, coaxes the best out of each other.

The way Dan loves me.

He cocks his head to the side in silent question. I rise to my toes and kiss him on the lips. "I love you."

I adore the feel of his smile against my mouth.

"I love you too."

Pam helps lead the charge with the guests, asking everyone to move their chairs to the round tables at the rear of the room for the reception. A handful of residents who formed a jazz band a few years ago set up their instruments where the bride and groom said their vows minutes ago. Dad and Paige roll up the aisle runner, and then it's time for phase two.

Silas leads Peggy to the dance floor as the band plays the intro to "Can't Help Falling in Love." That song was the best thing to come out of *Blue Hawaii*, in my opinion, though I'd never tell Peggy so. The bandleader is no Elvis, but he does the song justice as the bride and groom sway in each other's arms, gazes locked in pure adoration.

So many feelings, y'all. It's too much.

"Hey," Dan says, touching my elbow and guiding me outside.

There, away from the throng of people, away from the tidal wave of emotion, I can breathe.

I suck in a lungful of cold afternoon air, closing my eyelids as I turn my face toward the warm glow of the sun. Opening again, my heart stutters at the love and concern in Dan's gaze.

"Thank you," I whisper. "You knew exactly what I needed."

The side of his mouth tilts upward as he pulls me close. The strains of the song float on the breeze as Dan leads me into a graceful slow dance on the edge of the sidewalk outside the pool house. He hums along, carrying the melody as we sway.

We're interrupted by my phone alarm. I set them for each phase of the wedding in case my brain got hijacked, as it's prone to do.

"Come with me to oversee the dinner service?" I ask, offering Dan my hand.

His fingers twine with mine as we walk the path toward the main building. I shiver from the cold.

"Sorry, I forgot to bring a jacket," he says, as if he's somehow responsible for anticipating my every need, which is so silly and so sweet it warms me right up.

"It's fine. We'll be inside in a second."

He opens the door for me, and the first thing I notice at the end of the hall is the cluster of mistletoe. I raise my eyebrow but decide to leave it. The decorations are coming down tomorrow anyway.

Dan pauses beneath the cluster and kisses me, short and quick. He yanks the mistletoe, pockets it, and resumes walking with a satisfied smirk.

The next doorway boasts another sprig.

I'm pulled into another kiss, this one gentler, sweeter. Again, he removes the sprig and stuffs it into his pocket.

We turn toward the kitchens, and there I spot another green bunch. This one with a red bow.

As we pass beneath this time, I'm ready. Dan tugs me flush against him. I press my lips to his once, twice, three times before sinking into a languid kiss that prompts satisfied smiles on both our faces when we come up for air.

"Am I changing your opinion about the mistletoe yet?"

I grin. "Hmm. Might need more data."

His laughter fills the hall as he also pockets this sprig before nudging me forward. I nearly forgot we have a job to do.

The kitchen is abuzz with activity. They're loading two rolling carts with covered steamer pans. The chef calls out a greeting, assuring me they have everything under control and on its way to the pool house.

Dan leads me the opposite direction we came from.

"Where are we going? We need to get back," I protest.

"Trust me, will you?"

We stop and kiss under every single doorway.

And each time, he stops to collect the mistletoe.

"What are you doing? I'll get those tomorrow when I take down the Christmas stuff."

"Quit thinking so hard, and help me," he says when we enter the front reception area where there are multiple doorways branching off in all directions. I have to jump to pull down the sprigs, so it takes me twice as long. We meet at the entrance to the hallway between the storage room and my office.

His hands are full and so are his pants pockets. The tiny pockets in my maxi dress are too. Dan digs into one pocket and removes a small keyring, unlocking the storage room door.

He grabs the bucket from the top shelf. The very *empty* bucket.

My eyes widen as he begins filling it with the sprigs we've collected. I'm so dumb. Should've caught on way sooner.

"You did this?"

He replaces the bucket on the shelf, grabs me by the hand, and leads me toward my office.

"Are you mad?"

I pause to consider. "I might've been if I'd discovered it last week."

He grins the sexiest grin, and I'm tempted to kiss his face off without the mistletoe. Maybe because of it.

I do need to know, though.

"Why?"

"Because I knew it would drive you crazy. And we both know I live for that."

Shaking my head, I can't fight the laugh building inside me from the sheer joy this man brings to my life. I'm a mess without him. But with him, I can do anything. Or nothing.

I can just be.

That's no small thing.

He opens my office door and tilts my chin up. Sure enough, on the inside of the frame is one last green and white cluster.

Dan reaches up to remove it, but I stay his hand.

"Don't mess with that one."

His lips tip upward into a half smile as he leans closer until we're a breath apart. "You sure?"

"Yes. You've changed my opinion about mistletoe," I say with a nod, letting my nose caress the side of his as the moment stretches and the anticipation builds. "Besides, I have a feeling we're going to be making good use of it for a long, long time."

"Say, the next fifty or sixty years?" he asks, coming closer until I can't take it any longer.

"At least. Now please, for the love of Christmas, kiss me."

THE END

Not ready to say goodbye to Alessia and Dan? Curious about the grotesque cat figurine Dan purchased at the craft fair? Subscribe to Jaycee's monthly emails to receive an exclusive BONUS SCENE!

https://jayceeweaver.com/newsletter

acknowledgments

Not every book becomes an instant favorite, but for me, this one absolutely has. It's been a long, hard road back to writing since the fall of 2021 when that virus we all hate tried so hard to kill me. After my hospitalization, I spent most of 2022 recovering on oxygen—barely able to walk, let alone create. I managed to put out one semi-okay novella for a collection with friends and spent the rest of the year struggling to finish the final Sinclair Sisters book. It became clear by the start of 2023 that I was suffering pretty serious burnout too. Could I even write anymore? Did I want to? Was this going to be yet another hobby I'd once been passionate about only to abandon when I lost interest?

Praise God the answer to that last question was no. And without a doubt, all credit for being able to finish this book and fall in love with the characters belongs to Him. I wasn't so sure I liked Alessia until about 1/3 of the way in when I realized how much of myself I'd poured into her. After cringing, second guessing that maybe she was a little too all over the place, a little too much, a little too rough around the edges, I realized that this girl needed what I've always needed. What all women who'd been told those things their whole lives need: someone to accept her AS IS as she learns to own the weird ways her brain works. Now, Dan? I loved that guy from page one.

There are always a lot of people to thank after writing a book, and I'm especially blessed to have a truly wonderful team supporting me! Eric, K, A, and L, thank you for putting up with my disappearing acts as the deadline loomed closer and closer. You're my favorites and I love you to pieces. Thanks to Toni Shiloh and Teresa Tysinger for your critiques during the entire writing process. I write better when I have an audience, apparently. Ha ha! A huge thanks also to Jenn, Deena, Allyson, and Gretchen for your early feedback and spotting all the typos I missed!

Thank YOU, reader, for choosing to spend your time with another of my books.

Thanks especially to Sophia Walsh for your keen editing skills and excellent taste in selecting promo quotes! I'm sorry for all those rampant comma splices. I'll work on splitting my sentences instead of rambling on for eternity. LOL!

Lastly, thanks to my Creator for giving me the ability and drive to tell stories that inject a bit of light and fun into this dark and hurting world. Everything I write is for Your glory, and I praise Your name forever!

When New Mexico resident and USA Today bestselling author Jaycee Weaver isn't reading or writing, she enjoys dates with her brainiac hubby, drinking coffee, crafting, pretending she's a nature photographer, and making her teenagers cringe.

Jaycee considers herself a recovering perfectionist and frequent hot mess. She does her best to live her faith in action authentically, trusting God to be Lord over the good, the bad, and the ugly even when it's hard.

You can check out more of Jaycee's books or join her online community via her website, www.jayceeweaver.com.

Manufactured by Amazon.ca
Acheson, AB